IT IS LOVE

Quickly they left the drawing room and slipped into the dimly lit library.

Then she was in his arms, kissing him as fervently as he was kissing her.

"Everything's going to be all right," she murmured. "As long as we still love each other, nothing can go wrong. Let's get married very soon."

"My darling Verna, you are so brave. If only I had your courage."

"It comes from you. Oh, kiss me, kiss me!"

He did so, pulling her hard against him and putting his whole heart and soul into the kiss.

For a few blinding moments they were transported through the stars to Heaven.

But then, as he had always known would happen, Heaven was snatched away by an ominous sound.

The click of the library door closing.

Looking up, Michael saw with a sinking heart that Lord Challoner had come into the room and was standing there watching them with cold hard eyes.

"You must forgive me for intruding," he remarked tartly, "but I do have the strongest objection to having my daughter seduced under my roof."

"Papa!" Verna burst out indignantly.

"Be silent!" her father snapped at her. "You should be ashamed to behave like this, throwing yourself at him."

THE BARBARA CARTLAND PINK COLLECTION

Titles in this series

IT IS LOVE

BARBARA CARTLAND

Barbaracartland.com Ltd

THE BARBARA CARTLAND PINK COLLECTION

Barbara Cartland was the most prolific bestselling author in the history of the world. She was frequently in the Guinness Book of Records for writing more books in a year than any other living author. In fact her most amazing literary feat was when her publishers asked for more Barbara Cartland romances, she doubled her output from 10 books a year to over 20 books a year, when she was 77.

She went on writing continuously at this rate for 20 years and wrote her last book at the age of 97, thus completing 400 books between the ages of 77 and 97.

Her publishers finally could not keep up with this phenomenal output, so at her death she left 160 unpublished manuscripts, something again that no other author has ever achieved.

Now the exciting news is that these 160 original unpublished Barbara Cartland books are already being published and by Barbaracartland.com exclusively on the internet, as the international web is the best possible way of reaching so many Barbara Cartland readers around the world.

The 160 books are published monthly and will be numbered in sequence.

The series is called the Pink Collection as a tribute to Barbara Cartland whose favourite colour was pink and it became very much her trademark over the years.

The Barbara Cartland Pink Collection is published only on the internet. Log on to www.barbaracartland.com to find out how you can purchase the books monthly as they are published, and take out a subscription that will ensure that all subsequent editions are delivered to you by mail order to your home.

NEW

Barbaracartland.com is proud to announce the publication of ten new Audio Books for the first time as CDs. They are favourite Barbara Cartland stories read by well-known actors and actresses and each story extends to 4 or 5 CDs. The Audio Books are as follows:

The Patient Bridegroom	The Passion and the Flower
A Challenge of Hearts	Little White Doves of Love
A Train to Love	The Prince and the Pekinese
The Unbroken Dream	A King in Love
The Cruel Count	A Sign of Love

More Audio Books will be published in the future and the above titles can be purchased by logging on to the website www.barbaracartland.com or please write to the address below.

If you do not have access to a computer, you can write for information about the Barbara Cartland Pink Collection and the Barbara Cartland Audio Books to the following address:

Barbara Cartland.com Ltd., Camfield Place,
Hatfield, Hertfordshire AL9 6JE, United Kingdom.
Telephone: +44 (0)1707 642629
Fax: +44 (0)1707 663041

THE LATE DAME BARBARA CARTLAND

Barbara Cartland who sadly died in May 2000 at the age of nearly 99 was the world's most famous romantic novelist who wrote 723 books in her lifetime with worldwide sales of over 1 billion copies and her books were translated into 36 different languages.

As well as romantic novels, she wrote historical biographies, 6 autobiographies, theatrical plays, books of advice on life, love, vitamins and cookery. She also found time to be a political speaker and television and radio personality.

She wrote her first book at the age of 21 and this was called *Jigsaw*. It became an immediate bestseller and sold 100,000 copies in hardback and was translated into 6 different languages. She wrote continuously throughout her life, writing bestsellers for an astonishing 76 years. Her books have always been immensely popular in the United States, where in 1976 her current books were at numbers 1 & 2 in the B. Dalton bestsellers list, a feat never achieved before or since by any author.

Barbara Cartland became a legend in her own lifetime and will be best remembered for her wonderful romantic novels, so loved by her millions of readers throughout the world.

Her books will always be treasured for their moral message, her pure and innocent heroines, her good looking and dashing heroes and above all her belief that the power of love is more important than anything else in everyone's life.

"The moment your heart tells you that you are in love is the most divine and magical moment for anyone and you will remember the wonder of it for the rest of your life."

Barbara Cartland

CHAPTER ONE
1899

A few miles from Paris the road curved and they were bowling along on the last stretch through the country under the trees.

"We should be reaching the house very soon," Lady Verna remarked, looking about eagerly.

"Don't you worry, mademoiselle," replied Gaston, her driver. "I know where we are going."

The car was a magnificent machine, the very latest model from the Daimler factory. Gaston loved driving it, but he was very conscious that it did not belong to him.

He was simply the hired driver for the spirited and decisive young English lady who sat in the passenger seat beside him.

She had a definite air about her that came only from belonging to the aristocracy. She was charming, but it was clear that she was used to having her own way.

She was also very pretty, dressed in the very latest fashion of travelling wear for ladies.

Her jacket and skirt were deep blue, nipped in to a tiny waist. Underneath the jacket was a pale blue blouse, heavily decorated with embroidery and lace.

On her head she wore a large hat, anchored down with a luxuriant veil that tied under her chin.

Gaston had accepted the job of driving her and her

stern-faced chaperone from Calais to this house, because it afforded him a free journey to visit his fiancée.

"Are you all right back there, Winifred dear?" Lady Verna called over her shoulder.

"I'm managing," came the unpromising reply.

Verna glanced back to smile at the woman who had been her nurse and companion for years.

Although quite elderly, Winifred let nothing come between her and what she saw as her duty – accompanying her headstrong young Mistress here, there and everywhere.

Whenever possible she tried to stand between Lady Verna and disaster – not an easy task as the young lady had a passion for adventure and no sense of fear.

For instance it had seemed to her perfectly natural to travel to France to visit her brother Andrew and to do so in her father's brand new Daimler.

They had travelled to Dover, crossed the channel by ferry and at Calais she had calmly hired a driver.

'Thank goodness,' Winifred sighed to herself, 'we would soon reach the house and her brother would then be responsible for her.'

Soon they were turning into the gates of the little estate Andrew had inherited from a French aunt three years ago and where he had lived ever since.

And there he was on the steps to welcome them.

Except that his first words to Verna were not at all welcoming.

"What the devil are you doing here?"

"Charming, brother dear," exclaimed Verna. "I am as delighted to see you – as you are to see me!"

His petulant face settled into a scowl.

"All right," he sulked, "I didn't mean it to sound like that."

2

"What did you mean?" Verna asked, accepting his help to descend. "You knew I was coming to visit you."

"You said you would be driving the car down here at some time, so that I could have a look at it. You were vague about when. Now I have to rush off."

"Have to – or want to?" she asked.

She knew her brother only too well and he never did anything that did not suit him.

"I've had an invitation to make a long visit with the Solozzi family," he said awkwardly, "and I'm about to go."

"But they live in Rome," she protested.

"That's where I am going – to Rome. Look Verna, this is very important to me. They have a daughter. She is very pretty and very – well – "

"Very rich?"

"Money is useful and this house is very expensive."

"But you cannot leave when I have just arrived."

"I have to. They are expecting me."

"And just what am I supposed to do?" she cried in outrage.

"I suppose you could come with me," he suggested reluctantly.

"What an irresistible invitation!"

"Well, I don't really think that you would enjoy it. Perhaps you had better go home. Is this your driver?"

He indicated Gaston.

"Yes, he brought me from Calais, but – "

"Naturally I'll pay him to take you back."

"No, monsieur," piped up Gaston, shaking his head firmly. "I very much regret, but no."

"What on earth do you mean?" Andrew demanded, incensed at this defiance.

3

"Gaston's family live in this area and he only drove me here because he wants to spend some time with them," explained Verna.

"Oh, what nonsense, it's just a question of paying enough. I don't mind that."

But Gaston firmly stood his ground, something that Andrew did not understand.

"Just tell me how much," he snapped.

"He has already told you he is not driving back to Calais," Verna persisted, becoming indignant on Gaston's behalf. "I can drive myself."

"No, you cannot," Gaston said unexpectedly. "You know that in this country you need a licence to drive a car. I have one, but you do not and you said that was why you needed me at Calais."

"Yes – " agreed Verna reluctantly. "In England we don't need them. But perhaps – just for one journey – "

"*No*," exclaimed Gaston.

"Then *you* will have to drive her back to Calais."

"No, he won't, Andrew. That's not fair. Gaston, will you take me as far as Paris? It's only a short distance and there I can find another driver, and you can return to your family and your fiancée."

Gaston agreed to this suggestion after a long pause.

Andrew was so relieved to have the matter settled without trouble to himself that he ceased his objections, and even invited his sister to come into the house.

"But don't stay too long. It will be dark soon."

"Don't worry, you won't have to invite us for the night," replied Verna, feeling thoroughly sick of him. "We will have tea and then we'll depart."

*

4

On the way back to Paris, Gaston proposed,

"I will leave you at the best hotel in Paris. They will have drivers to take you back to Calais."

He was as good as his word, seeing her safely into the *Hotel Belle Epoque*, where she was able to book rooms for herself and Winifred. She paid his fee with something extra to cover his journey home, and assured him that she would manage very well from now on.

"After all, I have Winifred to protect me!"

Having fully experienced Winifred's sharp tongue, Gaston shuddered and departed.

"What a really lovely place," smiled Verna, looking around at her lavishly furnished room. "I think I will wear my best gown for dinner tonight."

"But you have nobody to dine with," said Winifred.

"I will sit at my table in the dining room and all the gentlemen will look at me – "

"They will not, my Lady, you will have supper sent up here like a respectable woman. The idea of you being ogled by strange men and talking about it like that – *well*!"

In the end she had her own way and they dined in Verna's room.

"I suppose I should be glad of it," Verna admitted. "It's been a long journey, starting out at five o'clock in the morning, catching the ferry, finding somewhere to stay for the night in Calais and then spending two days on the road, going to Andrew's place. We've hardly had a proper meal since we started."

She yawned.

"I suppose I should have told them at reception that I want a driver to Calais, but I cannot be bothered now. I'll do it in the morning. I am sleepy and an early night will do us both good."

"Hmm!" Winifred muttered rather cynically. She was never more suspicious than when Verna was docile.

"What do you mean by 'hmm' in that doom-laden voice?"

"I mean 'hmm'. When you talk just like a sensible woman, it always means that you're planning mischief!"

Verna chuckled in a way that filled her companion with foreboding.

"But life is much more fun if you have a sense of adventure," she insisted.

"You have too much sense of adventure," Winifred declared firmly. "You are now twenty-five and it's time you were married."

Verna made a face.

"Everyone says that. According to them I should make a suitable match with a suitable Lord and have a pack of suitable children!"

"Exactly."

"But none of the Lords I have met strike *me* as at all suitable," protested Verna. "Some of them are too old, some are too young and they are all dead bores."

"They are gentlemen of your own class, which is important."

"And because they are from my class I have known them all my life. *They* never do anything unexpected and if *I* do something unexpected, it scares them rigid!

"If only I could meet someone who was completely different. But I won't and you know why? Because there isn't anyone completely different. It's a myth – like the unicorn."

"Good!" declared Winifred. "The last thing I need is having to cope with you running off with a unicorn!"

"I'll never be able to find a unicorn," Verna replied despondently. "It's a dream that will end in nothing. I'll marry an Earl and become a Countess. I'll become boring and middle-aged like all Countesses, and that will be the end of me. Oh dear, oh dear, oh dear!"

She sighed.

Life was suddenly very depressing.

*

Michael Belmont yawned as he woke up.

He forced his eyes open as he knew that he would be offended by the sight of the shabby room where he was now forced to live.

The windowpane was cracked, the wallpaper dirty and there was a general air of melancholy.

Nobody looking at his squalid surroundings would realise that he was Viscount Larne, the eldest son and heir of the Earl of Belmont.

He groaned as he recalled the previous night when he had gone to the casino, determined to win back some of the money he had lost.

And, as often before, he had not only drunk far too much, but had again lost a great deal of money.

He thought, as he usually did, that he was the most unlucky man alive.

Whether he gambled on horses or cards, he seldom won so much as a penny and his rare winnings did not stay with him very long.

'Why am I such a fool,' he asked himself yet again, 'as to keep on gambling, although I know that I am bound to lose, as the Gods are against me?'

He realised that why he had so over-indulged last night was because he was tired and needed sustenance.

But to drink brandy always gave him a bad feeling the following morning.

His mind ranged back over the last few days, since he had arrived in Paris.

At first he had put up at an expensive hotel, suitable to his position. His valet had been with him and for a short time he had lived well.

But a few nights at the casino had severely depleted his funds and he had been forced to leave his hotel while he still had enough to pay the bill.

To save money he had sent his valet home and had moved into a cheap *pension*, a down-at-heel place where he could live frugally until his luck turned.

He was quite convinced that it would happen any day, but mysteriously, it never did.

He continued to lose, occasionally winning enough to keep his hopes alive, but never enough to cover his total losses and he did not even like to think of what those losses must be by now.

The previous evening he had been overtaken by a kind of rage that had impelled him to stake more and more, refusing to accept that luck was against him.

'My father was right,' he thought gloomily. 'I am good for nothing, just as he said.'

And yet he had not always been like that.

He recalled happy years at home while his mother had been alive. They had always been close and her death had shattered him. But what had made his grief worse was his father's behaviour.

Lord Belmont had never been a faithful husband, but at least he had been discreet about his affairs, but his wife's death had been the trigger for a wild burst of self-indulgence.

He had taken mistress after mistress, flaunting them before Society, even taking them back to Belmont Park, his ancestral home, and allowing them to occupy the room that had once belonged to his wife.

In disgust Michael had fled, seeking forgetfulness in dissipation. He too had known too many women of the wrong sort and then he had developed a taste for gambling.

After all, he reasoned, why not? His inheritance was vast. It would be well-nigh impossible for one man to go through it all.

But his father had been completely outraged.

He had no objection to women or drunken orgies. A gentleman of Society was expected to indulge himself.

But losing money was a different matter.

He had summoned his son home and they had had a serious quarrel, which ended in Michael fleeing the house yet again.

Lord Belmont threatened to cut off his allowance, and Michael had retorted that it would make no difference.

"You cannot incur debts if you have no means of paying," the Earl had snarled.

Michael had just shrugged his shoulders. His father would pay off his debts, no matter how much, for fear of a stain on the family name.

He had won in advance and they both knew it.

"Get out," the Earl yelled. "Get out of my sight."

Michael had obliged willingly and for the next five years he had lived the life of a gambler and libertine, as indifferent to his father's opinions as to the world's.

His French friends introduced him to casinos and congratulated him warmly if he was a winner.

The French women invariably welcomed him into their houses and, sometimes, their beds.

He was delighted to spend both the days and nights with them because they not only found him attractive, but never hesitated to say so nor were they shocked at anything he said or did.

Thus fortified he decided he could afford to ignore the opinions of his family.

He told himself that he was also indifferent to his own opinion, but secretly he knew that was not true.

His life was nothing but a wild attempt to overcome a terrible feeling of futility, but always at the back of his mind was a little nagging voice that said things might have been different – might have been so much better.

Depressed, he allowed his thoughts to dwell on his last visit to Belmont Park.

His father had confronted him in a fury.

"Debts and more debts," he thundered. "I suppose you think you will pay them off from your inheritance, but you won't get another penny out of me, not even when I am dead."

Michael had fled back to France, determined to stay there and was welcomed into the country house of friends who had just bought their first horseless carriage, the new toy that Society was raving about – the motor car.

"It'll never catch on," Michael had scoffed. "You will never replace horses with *that thing*."

But the moment he was seated behind the wheel a transformation had come over him and when the vehicle started he was filled with delight.

Soon the whole family were laughing at him as he became the horseless carriage's most fervent enthusiast.

As soon as he could drive well enough, he applied for a driving licence, which had been obligatory in France since 1896 and succeeded with flying colours.

He planned to buy his own car, but he could never decide between the new models that kept being produced.

In the meantime his finances continued to dwindle and his attempts to revive them at the Paris gaming tables never succeeded.

Down and down he had slid, only vaguely aware of his descent, but not quite knowing what to do about it.

Now he hauled himself up in bed to look again at the newspaper he had taken from a table downstairs when he had struggled back last night.

He only had to look at his evening coat on the floor and his trousers thrown half onto a chair to remember that he had drunk too much.

He had not even been able to read the paper and so had flung it on the floor.

Now he made an effort to concentrate on the words.

Suddenly he grew tense at what he read.

His father was dead.

He read it again and again before he was, at last, convinced that it was true.

His father, the Earl, had died the previous week. The funeral was being delayed while a search was mounted for his eldest son – who had vanished.

Michael sat, stunned.

The very last words his father had ever spoken to him were to express his anger and disapproval of him.

Now they would never see each other again.

But surely that was impossible.

How could his father, who had always quarrelled with him and who had said he was a disgrace to the family, just vanish from the face of the earth?

Then the truth struck him.

11

He was now the Earl of Belmont.

'I must go home at once,' he muttered. 'They are looking for me. How could I be such an irresponsible fool as to vanish and tell nobody where I was?'

He rubbed his eyes, wishing his head did not ache so.

'But that is all in the past,' he added. 'From now on, I shall have to live differently. I must start the journey home at once.'

But how?

He froze as yet another truth hit him.

He had almost no money. Once he had paid for his room, he would not be able to afford the journey.

'Why the hell was I such a fool?' he asked himself.

But he knew there was no real answer.

'I will have to borrow the money somehow. After all I am the Earl now. It should not be too hard to raise a loan from one of my friends or even a bank.'

He groaned when he thought of his bad reputation.

Who would ever want to lend money to Michael Belmont, knowing it would probably never be returned?

But for *Lord* Belmont, maybe it would be different.

He began to get ready, wishing his valet was here to help him. Shaving was difficult, but at last he managed it. He had a poor selection of clothes, having pawned most of them. His best attire was his evening dress, which he kept for the casino, but he could hardly wear that today.

He did possess a morning suit, which should have made him appear respectable, but it had clearly seen better days. His valet might have kept it looking smart, but it still looked a bit shabby.

But there was nothing else he could possibly do, so he donned the morning suit, wondering if anyone would lend him money once they had seen it.

He was far from pleased by his appearance.

It was not the right way for the new Lord Belmont to claim his inheritance, but it would have to do.

Running downstairs, he went out into the street and headed across Paris to the smart part of the City.

He was seeking the *Hotel Belle Epoque*, where he was on excellent terms with Pierre, the receptionist, after giving him a successful racing tip. Pierre would allow him to borrow the services of one of the hotel valets.

But outside the hotel he paused, riveted by the sight of a motor car that was parked outside.

This was not just a motor car.

It was the most modern beautiful machine he had ever seen. It seemed to sing to him from a distance – and he followed the call.

For several minutes he walked round and round the exquisite article, his senses reeling with admiration.

It had what he had never seen before – back seats. Every car he had ever driven had just two seats, one for the driver and one for a passenger. But this one could take two more passengers in the rear.

Whatever would they think of next?

He looked for the owner, peering into the hotel.

A lady was standing at the desk, talking to Pierre, who was listening to her with a furrowed brow.

Michael noticed she was wearing a hat with a large veil, the kind ladies often wore when they were travelling in a car to protect them from the wind.

He walked up to the desk and heard her speaking French with some difficulty. Obviously she was English.

He listened to her and was amazed.

She was trying to explain that she wanted to hire a capable driver to drive her to Calais and from there she would catch a ferry to Dover. Once in England she would take over the wheel herself and drive home.

'She intends to drive this fabulous car herself!' he thought, thunderstruck. 'But ladies just did *not* do that.'

It was obvious that Pierre was finding it difficult to understand her. He shrugged repeatedly, implying that she was asking for the moon.

"But there must be someone," the young lady stated desperately. "I thought such a good hotel would employ drivers or at least know where they are to be found."

"I will try to find your Ladyship the sort of driver you want," Pierre replied in French. "But our drivers only cover short distances in the City. We do not have anyone suitable for you at the moment."

"Then you must find someone for me and quickly!" she demanded. "I have to go back to England."

She spoke decisively and Michael could not repress a smile. He was not normally an admirer of very decisive ladies. He preferred them soft and fluttery – but this one was charming.

Acting on impulse, he addressed her in English,

"I wonder if I can help you."

Swiftly she turned round and he had a glimpse of a pair of dazzling blue eyes set in a sweet heart-shaped face.

Michael drew a long slow breath, feeling the world spin around him. At last it settled back into place.

But not the same place.

Looking at this glorious girl, he knew that nothing would ever be the same again.

CHAPTER TWO

"Can I help you in any way?" he repeated.

"Oh, you're English!" she exclaimed. "Please make this man understand that I have to go home immediately, and I need a driver to take me as far as Calais. After that I can manage."

"You certainly should not be stranded here in Paris all alone."

"I am not alone. Winifred is with me."

She glanced over to a far corner where there sat a large elderly woman, glaring at the world and, seemingly, at Michael in particular.

"She is your *only* protection?" he asked, astounded.

"I don't really need protection. I am quite capable of looking after myself," the girl asserted firmly.

She was really such a dainty little thing, so pretty and vulnerable and yet so blithely confident that she could make the world do her bidding that Michael felt a tug on his heart strings.

"But I really need help with this car," she carried on. "When I came abroad previously my father has always been with me – "

She added in a confiding voice,

"I am not a particularly good driver."

Even this remark she managed to make sound like a good joke. But Michael, who could not imagine that any

15

woman was ever a good driver, was beginning to consider her in need of care and protection.

"Then Heaven seems to have sent me to you," he said. "I have to return to England myself right now, so perhaps I can drive you."

He thought he saw a flash of relief in her face, but it was quickly quenched and replaced by uncertainty.

Her eyes flickered over his appearance and he now realised that she was worried by his shabby clothes. For all she knew, he might be a ne'er-do-well.

Which in a sense he was, he thought wryly.

"Please don't be in any way alarmed," he hastened to say. "After all your maid is here to act as chaperone. I shall be little more than a servant, yours to command – "

Her eyes brightened.

"Would you really drive me home?" she asked. "It would be very kind of you."

"Why don't we sit down to talk this over. There is a queue building up behind us."

She glanced behind her and gave a guilty start.

"Yes, you are quite right. We are holding everyone up and they look rather cross."

They moved away to a table with two empty seats. Here the light was a bit better and Michael could see that she was even prettier than he had at first thought.

"I was admiring your motor car before I came in. I have never seen the like before."

"It's a Daimler," she told him. "The firm has only just brought it out and my Papa bought one of the first."

"And he lets you drive it?" enquired Michael with an involuntary emphasis of astonishment.

He knew he had made a mistake when he saw the sparkling annoyance in her eyes.

"And why, pray, should Papa not let me drive it?"

"No reason at all," he amended hastily.

"Are you one of those old-fashioned stick-in-the-mud men who think women belong only in the home, and should never be allowed outside to do anything interesting? Because if so, let me tell you – "

How glorious she was, he pondered, dazed and not hearing a word. He was well past listening, past anything except thinking just how amazingly lucky he was that this heavenly creature had crossed his path.

"So just what do you think of that?" she asked him triumphantly.

He came out of his blissful dream.

"I beg your pardon?"

"I asked what arguments you might have to refute mine, but of course you were not listening."

"But I was," he replied, crossing his fingers. "You are so right. Too many men will take a blinkered view of women, but I gather that your father is not one of them."

"Papa likes his children to share his enthusiasms. I was reared like my brothers and I can do anything they do. Play golf, drive a car, ride a horse!"

"And I'll wager that you do these things as well as they."

She looked shocked.

"As well as – ?"

"I mean that, of course, you do them better."

"Of course," she agreed, her lovely face full of fun.

"I beg your pardon, ma'am."

Their eyes met.

17

Mutual understanding glowed between them and it filled him with a pleasant irrational happiness.

"I meant to drive all the way here," she added, "but I don't have a licence to drive in France, so I hired a driver at Calais. All went very well until I reached my brother Andrew's house, just south of Paris.

"He heard about the new Daimler and wrote to say he wanted to see it, so Papa said I could drive it down to show him. But when I arrived I found that he was about to depart for Italy. My driver didn't want to leave the area, so he could not take me back to Calais.

"He did bring me to Paris last night, so that I could find someone else. But so far I have been unlucky."

"Well, I would be very delighted to drive your car to Calais and since I am also going to England, I can come further with you."

"Thank you very much, sir. I am so grateful."

A thought seemed to strike her.

"Perhaps we should introduce ourselves. I am Lady Verna Langham, eldest daughter of Lord Challoner."

The name Challoner was familiar to Michael.

The family lived a few miles from Belmont Park, but his father had said they were not worth knowing. This suggested a falling out, which did not surprise him as his testy father fell out with many people.

He might well have met this delightful young lady years ago, instead of only now. How different would that have made things?

"And my name is Michael Payne," he said, giving his mother's maiden name.

It would be a mistake, he considered, to say his real name and to let her know that he was now the Earl. There would be explanations enough later.

"Do you think we could leave quickly?" she asked.

"Yes, I – I must return to my hotel first."

"Let me drive you there."

"No thank you," he said with a horrified picture of her face if she should see the wretched hole he was staying in. "I will return in an hour. Where is your luggage?"

"It is here in this hotel, where I stayed last night."

"Then we should be able to make a quick start as soon as I return. Goodbye until then – "

As he hurried back to his hotel Michael's brain was working furiously. By the time he arrived he had made a desperate decision.

He was going to escape without paying his bill!

It was shocking, something that Society would call deeply dishonourable, but Society would not know about it and he would send the money as soon as he was in England and had assumed his inheritance.

'I couldn't pay it anyway,' he reasoned to himself. 'I just don't have enough money. But if I can sell my good evening clothes, I may just have enough to survive on the journey.'

He managed to get to his room without being seen and hastily packed a small suitcase with his evening wear. This was all he dared to take with him.

Slowly he opened his door and looked out into the corridor. When he saw that nobody was about, he crept out and closed the door very quietly behind him.

He held his breath. If anyone saw him they would know that he was fleeing, as he was carrying his suitcase.

He reached the top of the stairs.

One step, then another, and a few more brought him to where he could see the hall.

To his immense relief it was empty. He descended the last steps quickly and hurried out of the door. All the time he expected to hear someone call out "*arretez-vous*!"

But nobody did and he escaped.

As he hurried down the street, he realised that the die was cast. He had done a terrible thing. He was almost a criminal.

Now there was no going back.

He ran on to the local pawnshop and the man at the counter grinned when he saw him.

"What is it this time, monsieur?" he asked.

Michael laid out the suit on the counter.

"I want to sell it outright. How much?"

There followed some hard bargaining. In the end he had to settle for less than he needed, but he knew it was all he was going to receive.

As he hurried to the *Hotel Belle Epoque*, he had a terrible fear that Lady Verna would not be there. Perhaps it had all be a wild crazy dream!

But when he entered the lobby of the hotel he saw her immediately. She was sitting with Winifred and they seemed to be having an argument.

Suddenly Verna looked up and saw him. Her face brightened in a smile.

"At last," she called out. "Winifred, this is Michael Payne, the man who has come to save us."

Winifred glared, looking him up and down in a way that showed that she had noticed the shabbiness of his suit.

"How do you do," Michael bowed his head, leaning down to her with his most charming smile.

"Hrrmph!" was her only reply.

"Perhaps we should be on our way," he suggested. "Is this your luggage? Let me take it."

As he began to carry things out to the car, he heard the argument resumed behind him.

"You can't entrust yourself to that man," Winifred practically hissed. "You know nothing about him, except that he's a reprobate."

"He's not a reprobate – "

"Well, he certainly looks like one. Where does he come from? Who is he? No respectable gentleman would simply pop up from nowhere looking for a cheap journey."

He drew a sharp breath, reflecting that Winifred's judgement was too acute to be comfortable.

He loaded the car as quickly as possible, anxious to be off before Lady Verna allowed herself to be persuaded against him.

Finally they emerged, Winifred still scowling and clearly thinking the worst.

She made one last attempt to take charge.

"I think you should sit in the back, my Lady," she proposed. "And I will sit beside the driver. That will be more proper."

Quick as a flash, Michael handed Verna up into the front passenger seat, leaving Winifred fuming.

Then he held out his right hand to Winifred with an elegant flourish.

"Allow me to assist you, ma'am."

Not every gentleman behaved so politely to a mere companion, and even the formidable Winifred, that pillar of severe rectitude, was not immune to the courtesy or to Michael's charm, which he turned on in full measure.

She merely said, "Hmm!" glaring more fiercely, so that he should not suspect that she was softening, then took his hand and allowed him to help her up into the vehicle.

21

At last they were on their way, heading North out of Paris. Michael was glad to be leaving the City behind.

He had a vision of the manager of his hotel chasing after him, crying to the world that he had not paid his bill.

"How long did it take you to drive from Calais to Paris?" he asked Verna.

"Two days. We had to stay overnight in a little village. Unfortunately it isn't possible to make the journey in one day, not even by going very fast indeed."

"Did your driver go as fast as you wanted him to?" Michael enquired with a grin.

"No, he was very poor-spirited. He refused to go faster than ten miles an hour even on a clear country road."

"What a coward!" Michael exclaimed with feeling.

"That's what I thought. What's the point of having a car that can do a whole fifteen miles an hour if you don't take advantage of it?"

"Have you ever driven at such a speed?" he asked, growing more amused by the minute.

"No," she sighed with disappointment. "The most I have ever done is eight. But I was with Papa when he did ten. It was very exciting because he was stopped by the Police for speeding!"

"Good Heavens!"

"We were perfectly safe because there was nothing else on the road, but we were still technically within the town boundary, so the speed limit was two miles an hour.

"He was halted by an aggressive Policeman who said he would not tolerate people who behaved like a mad hooligan. Papa claimed that he was not a hooligan and the Policeman said the Magistrates would decide that. Then Papa took off his goggles and the Policeman recognised him as Lord Challoner.

"The man was horrified, but he stuck with his duty. He insisted that the law was the same for everyone. So Papa appeared in the Magistrates' Court and was fined for speeding. Now he has a criminal record and he is really proud of it. He keeps the paper framed on his wall and shows it to all his visitors!"

Michael roared with laughter.

"I think that he has missed the point," he spluttered when he could speak again. "You're not supposed to be proud of a criminal record!"

"No, but if you're Lord Challoner, you can afford to ignore convention," countered Verna. "That is – I didn't mean that to sound the way it did."

"How did it sound?" Michael asked puzzled.

He had just been thinking that his father had always adopted a similar attitude and when he himself assumed the title, he would probably do the same.

"I am afraid that people who boast a title tend to assume they are rather superior to others," she explained carefully. "Of course it isn't true, but we do it too easily."

"Are you trying to console me for my lack of a title?"

"Not exactly, I just didn't want you to think – that is – "

"That you are a superior female who look down on untitled men. Don't worry, I didn't think that."

He was fighting the temptation to tell her who he really was. In fact, he supposed it was his duty to abandon his deception, however innocently it had started.

But she was revealing a side of her nature that he found delightful and if she knew the truth, he would see it no more.

Just a little longer, he promised himself and then he would tell her the truth and never deceive her again as long as they lived.

23

With a shock he realised the way his thoughts had strayed. He had known her only a few hours, yet already he was thinking of a life together.

But how could he help it? he reasoned.

What man could resist her?

Certainly he could not.

Now they were out in the country, driving through beautiful scenery and Michael was aware of a feeling of blissful contentment.

Partly it was the sheer pleasure of handling such a modern motor car.

But partly it was the awareness of this heavenly girl beside him and the overwhelming sensation that a new and wonderful phase of his life was opening to him.

'The sooner I get home the better,' he thought to himself. 'There will be a great deal to do now I have to take Papa's place.'

Even to think about what lay ahead of him when he returned home made him long to cover the ground as fast as possible.

He drove on in silence for a while, concentrating on absorbing the feel of this marvellous machine.

But then Verna's soft voice interrupted his reverie,

"Do tell me what you have been doing in France."

With a major effort he pulled himself back to the present.

"Excuse me, I was thinking. What did you say?"

"I asked what you have been doing in France."

"Just – looking around Paris. What about you?"

"I came to visit my brother, as I told you. It's only since I have been here that I have realised how ignorant I am about France."

She gave a delightful laugh, adding,

"I suppose I know so very little about any European country except my own. When I get home I will have to make myself learn very much more."

"You will find it all fascinating, but after you have stayed in every country you will realise that home is best."

Verna laughed.

"I think that's what every Englishman feels."

"It's how I feel when I am at home in England. But there are plenty of interesting things to see in France and beautiful women to dance with and talk to."

"And doubtless, like so many Englishmen, you find French women irresistible," she teased.

Michael knew this to be true.

He had found many French women irresistible and they had felt the same about him, but it was not something he could say to this girl, so he made a non-committal reply and fell silent.

But she was not prepared to let the subject drop.

"Do you find French women more attractive than the English?" she asked him casually.

He tried to think of a suitable answer for her. He knew that many women were inclined to ask this kind of question and it made a man's life somewhat difficult.

If he was truthful, he would venture that he found French women much easier to flirt with than the average Englishwoman, who usually tried to run away.

But perhaps he should not say such a thing to a well bred girl, especially this one. Besides, when she knew who he really was, she might gossip about him.

He therefore ventured cautiously,

"I enjoy seeing other countries besides my own and

I have travelled quite a lot. In some countries a stranger is very welcome, but in others they are suspicious, especially of the English."

"That's very true," she responded thoughtfully.

"I always feel they are being careful when they talk to me, not only about my country but about theirs."

Michael laughed as he added,

"Perhaps you should stay in England and let people come to you rather than you going to them."

"That is more or less what my brother said to me. All the same he is now determined to enjoy himself with the Italians."

"Italian girls are very pretty," Michael commented solemnly. "Although not as pretty as the French."

She considered this broad statement for a moment, before enquiring in an impish voice,

"So you think French girls are prettier than those of any other country?"

Time to be cautious again, he mused.

Why ever did women insist on attempting to trap a man into an unwary statement?

At the same time he felt a sense of delight at her teasing and there was no doubt that she was very charming.

"When I am in France, I think the French girls are the prettiest in the world," he added tactfully. "And when in England I think the English girls are beyond compare!"

They both laughed and he exclaimed,

"You see what a diplomat I am!"

"Not at all. You have just insulted me."

"I have?"

"We are still in France, so obviously you think that French girls are prettier than I am."

"Ah, but we'll soon be in England," he came back quickly. "So I'm safe."

"Pardon me, sir. You will be safe when we reach England. Until then, I shall have to think of some suitable revenge!"

How enchanting she was, he thought. So lovely, so quick-witted.

"I will go in fear and trembling of your revenge," he riposted. "And I will say that I think someone as pretty and as young as you should never have been left alone in France – even though you were quite prepared to delegate the wheel to a mere male in order to get back to England!"

There was silence for a moment before Verna said,

"I must admit that if I had not found you, I don't know what I would have done."

Then she burst into laughter.

"And you will never know what that admission has cost me!"

He joined in her laughter, thinking how natural it was to laugh with her. She would fill his world with joy, he was certain.

"I think I can imagine what it cost you and I greatly appreciate your generosity. Now, why don't you tell me about yourself and why your brother has abandoned you in what I consider a rather unkind way, to say the least of it."

"He didn't consider it unkind. He never thinks of anything when he has an idea in his head. So he simply rushed off. I am afraid brothers are often like that."

Michael chuckled.

"I know just what you are saying. My sisters are always complaining about my selfishness."

"You have sisters?" Verna echoed eagerly. "Do tell me about them."

Cursing himself for this slip of the tongue, Michael continued,

"There is nothing to tell. I very rarely see them."

"Which accounts for them misunderstanding your character. For you are not selfish surely?"

A rare moment of shame held him silent.

"I am afraid I am – " he admitted at last.

"How can you be when you are so kind to me?"

"But I am gaining much from this myself – passage home and a chance to drive this wonderful car. I only hope I live up to your expectations."

"I think that you drive extremely well. This car is moving quicker and smoother than it did when my father was driving. Not that I would let him hear me say so."

"I will promise never to tell him that you were so uncomplimentary about his driving. That is – if I ever meet him," he amended hastily. "You must tell me where you live, so that I can drive you there."

"I think if you are kind enough to take me to my own country, I should then be able to drive myself home, if you have to go to London or somewhere else."

"I will take you home first," insisted Michael.

He was thinking he would have to be home in time for his father's funeral, but he could not simply abandon this delightful girl.

He would either have to find someone else to drive Lady Verna home or she would have to wait till the funeral was over.

But there was no point in saying all this just yet.

As he had no intention of talking about himself, he turned to Verna,

"Tell me some more about your brother. Why did he rush off to Italy like that?"

Verna gave a giggle.

"It is rather a strange story, but I expect, because you are a man, you will understand. My brother has been a huge success with a family of Italians who are very rich, who have – according to him – the most magnificent castle and some outstanding horses.

"They had invited him to stay on several occasions when he was unable to go. But when they learned we were in France, they were so insistent and made their invitation so fascinating that my brother simply couldn't refuse."

"But surely he wanted you to go with him?"

There was silence for a moment as if she felt the question was rather embarrassing.

"I have never met the friends he is with. Although he suggested I might go with him, I think he really wanted to go alone."

Michael chuckled.

"I think you spoil your brother."

"I am afraid we all do. He is very good-looking, charming and can be extremely amusing. In fact there are always women running after him. I knew if I did go with him, I should feel rather unnecessary."

"I know exactly what you mean, as I have often felt like that myself, but there is nothing you can do except try and pretend not to notice that you are not wanted."

"Yes, indeed," she replied with spirit, "and as I did not choose to be subjected to such a fate, I told him that I could easily drive myself home and that Winifred was all the company I needed."

"And he believed you?" he demanded, scandalised.

"He believed me because he wanted to believe me. Which is what most men do!"

This was true, he reflected. It was a sobering thought.

"But doubtless you will find that several handsome gentlemen are waiting for you in England – "

He was doing it himself he now realised – dropping hints, hoping for a response that would tell him something more about her.

But he could not help himself.

He did not know how long he might have with her and in that short time he must learn everything about her.

Suddenly he knew a moment of fear. Lady Verna had become more important than he had ever allowed any woman to be before.

It was frightening how much she mattered.

But then he knew that this response was unworthy of her.

He must throw off this fear and open his heart to whatever the future might bring.

He was smiling broadly as he drove onwards.

CHAPTER THREE

After a while Michael remarked, trying to sound nonchalant,

"You do not answer. I wonder why – "

"Because it does not concern *you*," came a caustic voice from the back seat.

Michael jumped.

He had forgotten about the dragon – as he thought of her – who was accompanying them.

"It is none of your business whether the young men at home are handsome," continued Winifred.

"Winifred, dear – " Verna protested mildly, looking back at her.

But Winifred had started and would not be stopped.

"Neither is it your business how many gentlemen there are," she stormed, "nor, indeed, if there are any at all!"

"But I'm sure that there are plenty," Michael added wickedly.

He was unable to resist teasing her.

"Just one quick look at Lady Verna tells me that the countryside around her house is bound to be filled with young gentlemen swooning with ecstasy."

Verna choked with laughter, covering her face with her hand.

"In fact," Michael continued, getting into his stride, "I am sure that Lady Verna – "

"Who are you to call her 'Lady Verna'?" Winifred broke in. "It's 'my Lady' to you."

In this way she informed him that he was no better than a servant in her eyes.

Michael, in a mood to find this amusing, supposed that he could not blame her.

"Oh, no," Verna added hurriedly. "Lady Verna will do very nicely."

"No, it won't," snapped Winifred.

"Yes, it will," Verna persisted firmly.

But she tempered her severity with a smile and her protective companion fell silent, contenting herself with a disapproving glare at Michael's back.

"Now," Verna resumed, returning her attention to him, "what were you saying?"

"Just that I wondered why you were so discreetly silent about your admirers – "

He half expected a thunderbolt to land on him, but Winifred had made her feelings plain and said no more – for the moment.

"There are many reasons as to why a woman might decline to discuss her admirers," Verna responded with a delicious smile that was modest and wickedly enticing at the same time.

"You mean she might have so many that she's lost count? I can hardly believe that."

"Or it may be the melancholy truth that she has no admirers at all – " Verna muttered soulfully.

But she gave him an impish look that dared him to believe her.

"Of course," he said, "she is a plain Jane, weeping into her pillow at night!"

Verna laughed, not in the least offended.

"Or she may not have decided amongst them. Such great decisions are not to be taken without much thought."

"Very true," Michael agreed sagely. "And she is a wise woman who does not rush into things."

A snort from behind him told them what Winifred thought of this opinion of her Mistress.

Michael grinned, whilst Verna glared.

"She is a *very* wise woman," Verna repeated firmly. "In fact she is known for her good sense."

Another snort.

"Her *great* good sense," Verna emphasised. "She has never done anything foolish in her life."

"Indeed?" Michael queried, sounding interested. "I heard a rumour that she dashed off to France in her car, got stranded and was forced to return to home by hiring some ne'er-do-well she found by pure chance. But I daresay that story is false."

"Totally false," Verna concurred primly.

"Now that's a pity, because I thought she sounded rather interesting."

There was a short pause as he waited for Winifred to strike him dead.

"Did you really?" Verna asked at last in a voice that gave nothing away.

"Indeed I did. Such a girl would be courageous, spirited, intelligent and extremely unusual. But – " he gave a melancholy sigh, "where is such a girl to be found? I am not sure that she exists anywhere in the world."

Verna said nothing and Michael had the feeling that for once something had bereft her of speech. He guessed that this was rare, but did not say so. He had tempted fate quite enough for one day.

After a while he probed,

"Of course, there is another possibility."

"What is that?" she asked in an uncertain voice.

"That she *has* decided among her suitors, but, for a while wishes to protect the identity of the favoured one."

"That is a possibility," she came back, and he could sense by her tone of voice that she had now recovered her composure and was back to teasing him.

"But I wonder if it's true – " he mused.

Silence.

Inside he was full of tension.

How had he managed to advance so quickly to the verge of disaster? For it would indeed be a disaster if there really was a man she loved.

Another moment would seal his fate.

Then he heard her laughing and the sound was like balm to his soul.

"If only my life was as interesting as you depict it, sir. The truth is that there are several young men in the neighbourhood, but I have known them all too long to be fascinated by them. Very sad, but there it is."

"What you are really telling me," asked Michael, speaking cautiously to conceal his relief, "is that you are looking for something new and exciting. It is rather like eating the same meal at the same time every single day and still expecting it to be enjoyable."

"That's a good way of describing it. One becomes bored with people one sees often, who say the same thing every day from Monday to Sunday."

"Quite right, Lady Verna" Michael agreed. "That's why we go abroad – for a variety of new sensations."

He fell silent, considering a few of the sensations he had found abroad.

'I'm now deceiving this charming girl,' he thought guiltily. 'What would she say if she knew what a reprobate I really am?'

"Is anything the matter?" she enquired, turning her head sideways to glance at his face.

"No, nothing," he murmured hurriedly. "We were talking about new sensations – "

"I am enjoying some at this very moment. I have never met you, but you have been kind enough to help me. I enjoy being with you and listening to your words, which are different from anything I have heard before."

"I might say the same to you," Michael responded. "After all, I expected, at this moment, to be travelling on a train. Instead of which I am driving a delightful and very expensive car with a very pretty and charming young lady, who has just jumped out from one of my dreams."

Verna laughed and clapped her hands.

"Excellent!" she exclaimed. "That is just the sort of thing you ought to say. If you were on a stage the whole audience would applaud!"

"That is most flattering, Lady Verna. Now, as we have travelled so far, I think you should tell me more about your family and much more about yourself."

"I'm sure everything I've done is dull compared to your life."

"A little dullness may not always be a bad thing," Michael observed, contemplating that perhaps his own life had sometimes been rather too over-exciting. "One does not want to be appearing in the newspapers."

"But if you are clever and are determined not to do anything which could make what they call 'a good story', there should be no danger."

"But perhaps I am not clever," Michael suggested.

"I refuse to believe it. I am sure that you are clever enough for anything."

'Of course,' he thought, 'a really clever man would not have been caught in Paris penniless. But then I would not have met this wonderful girl, so perhaps cleverness is a bit over-rated.'

"My mother always claimed that she considered it unnecessary to appear in the newspapers unless one was to be married or had died."

Verna giggled as she added,

"Otherwise everything we do know about ourselves should be kept secret – except from our relations and very special friends."

Michael laughed.

"Your mother was quite right. It is a great mistake for the newspapers to know too much, even though they try to listen at every door and peep through every keyhole."

"Of course they could easily make a story about us now," she muttered thoughtfully. "Such unconventional behaviour!"

That was true, he thought.

Fortunately nobody knew just how unconventional he had been. It was still unknown that he had inherited his father's title and been kind to a titled beauty.

As for running off without paying his hotel bill – that was unconventional to the point of being disgraceful. Any newspaper in England would jump on that story with delight.

But he only said,

"I promise I won't tell anyone how a beautiful lady came down from Heaven to take me on an adventure. And we will have to be Miss Brown and Mr. Jones, two people of absolutely no importance."

"You do think of everything," smlied Verna with a

contented sigh. "I know I can safely leave matters in your hands. Oh, I have been *so* lucky to find you."

In his heart he knew that he had another reason to feel lucky, one that he hardly dared to think of yet.

They stopped at a small village inn and had a quick lunch under Winifred's suspicious glare.

Michael was briefly concerned about paying for the meal, but Winifred insisted that it was her Ladyship's place to pay.

As she was speaking her eyes challenged Michael to dispute it. He meekly acquiesced, filled with relief, even though he knew she was underlining his lowly status.

As the meal ended Winifred became involved in a dispute with the waiter, whom she addressed in a mixture of English and basic French badly pronounced. When the poor man did not understand her, she raised her voice.

Verna took immediate advantage of the diversion to murmur hurriedly,

"I must apologise for Winifred's behaviour to you."

"It's perfectly all right," he smiled. "She insists on your paying because she wants me to understand that I'm only a servant. It doesn't matter."

"You are not a servant," she added warmly. "I can tell easily that you are a gentleman despite – " she broke off, embarrassed.

"Despite not looking like one!" he finished.

"Well, anyway, I naturally assume *all* the expenses of this trip as a way of showing my gratitude."

"That's very kind of you, but I'm not sure about *all* the expenses."

"But I am," she insisted. "I said all and I meant all. You are doing me a big favour and there is no reason why you should be out of pocket."

"But I had to return to England anyway – "

He could not imagine why he was protesting. Her attitude was a godsend to him and it would be a disaster if he was to win the argument.

But he could sense that there was no question of her giving in. He had never liked women of strong views, but her imperiousness was clearly a part of her charm and he was enjoying watching her eyes sparkle as she grew more determined.

"I am sure that I should make a contribution," he persisted, "even at the risk of convincing Winifred that I'm getting above myself."

"You will make *no* contribution. I have decided it is for me to pay and nobody else."

"But – "

"The matter is settled."

"Is it?" he asked lightly.

"Yes. It is."

"Perhaps I should call you – my Lady."

"I forbid it."

"Yes, my Lady."

"I said – " she caught him watching her and began to laugh.

He laughed too and somehow their hands touched.

Winifred having demolished the unfortunate waiter turned just in time to see it.

"We should be going," she announced resolutely.

*

In a few minutes they were on their way again and by late evening they had reached Amiens.

"We must stay here for the night," suggested Verna "You must be exhausted after driving for so long."

"I didn't want to stop while there was still light and now it's fading it won't be safe to drive on further. But we must ask them to call us at dawn tomorrow so that we can make an early start."

Someone directed them to a hotel two streets away.

Michael drove towards it slowly because by now he was indeed feeling very tired.

At the hotel he carried Verna's luggage inside and waited whilst she enquired about rooms. There were two rooms available, one double, one single.

"Winifred and I will share and you can have the single room."

"Thank you, but no," replied Michael. "I shall stay in the garage with the car tonight."

"But you can't sleep outside while I'm comfortable indoors," she protested.

"Why not?" growled Winifred. "That's a servant's place."

"Hush," Verna reproved her.

"I must stay with the car to make quite certain that no one tries to steal it," Michael persevered.

It was surely true, but it would also spare him the embarrassment of having her pay for his hotel room.

"I shall take the car out to their garage in a minute and stay there," he stated firmly.

"But you must come in for dinner – "

"No, but perhaps you will send me out something for me to eat and drink."

She did not answer for a moment. Secretly she was disappointed as she would have liked to have dined with him. Yet she knew he was right.

"I just hate to think of you having such a difficult night," she told him reluctantly.

She looked at Michael in such a gentle manner that he thought she was almost asking him to kiss her.

It was something he would certainly love to do, but he realised that he must restrain himself. Winifred would certainly strike him dead with her umbrella!

A porter showed him to the hotel garage, where the car would be safe. It was attracting much interest, which made Michael feel that he was wise to stand guard.

After a few minutes Verna appeared in the garage.

"I have ordered refreshments to be sent to you," she announced. "They will be here soon."

"Thank you so much."

"I told the Manager that your dinner must be of the best or there would be trouble,"

"I am sure you terrified him. You certainly terrify me!"

It was meant as a joke and he was surprised when she frowned in displeasure.

"I do wish people would stop making remarks like that, just because I know how to make up my mind," she complained.

"It's a gift that most young ladies don't have."

"I know and I have no patience with them all – silly creatures, always waiting for a man to tell them what to do and think. How absurd!"

He had been brought up in the belief that a truly feminine woman did indeed wait for a man to tell her what to think and he saw no reason to change now.

Nevertheless he nodded in the most weak-willed manner – it was the effect she had on him.

"As though we didn't have minds of our own – "

"Most young ladies are not taught to develop their minds," he reminded her.

"Well, I *have* been and I do not intend to change."

"*No*. You must never change."

Barely aware what he was doing, Michael took her hand in his and put it to his lips.

He kissed her fingers which were very soft and felt her tremble. Their eyes met and he thought again that he would have liked to kiss her lips.

Suddenly, as if she was afraid of what she could see in his eyes, she said,

"I'll go back to the hotel now as quickly as I can. I think you are – wonderful for staying out here – all night."

Her words seemed to tumble over each other and, almost as if she felt that she must run away, she turned and hurried towards the door.

He watched her until he could see her no longer.

Then he sat down in the car, deep in thought.

Things were moving so fast that he no longer knew exactly what was happening. It was like being in a fast car that had veered out of control. He did not know where he was going, he only knew that he did not want to jump off.

Wherever this wild journey might lead, he would stay on board until the end – as long as she was there too.

A few minutes later a man arrived with his meal. It was no mere snack, but a full dinner, everything a hungry man might need.

There was a note on the tray.

He read,

"*I have paid for all the food they have brought you, also tipped the man, so do not give him any more*

I hope you sleep comfortably as I will do."

It was signed with her name, all written in rather a scribble.

Michael was certain she had written it in a hurry. At the same time, he thought that this was exactly the kind of writing this unusual girl would have – wild, carefree and unconstrained.

He smiled, tucking the note away into his pocket. He would keep it as a souvenir.

He ate the meal, which was delicious and drank the excellent wine.

Then he was ready to go to sleep.

He removed his coat and his shoes as he felt more comfortable without them and then tried to settle down in the back seat, covered by the fur rug.

Gradually he began to fall asleep.

Verna's face seemed to float in his consciousness, reminding him how he had longed to kiss her.

He had a feeling, although he might be mistaken, that she would not have prevented him from doing so.

That was a shocking thing to think about a lady, but he hoped it was true!

It alarmed him how intensely he desired her kiss.

In another moment he was asleep.

The day's exertions had left him so exhausted that nothing would have woken him.

He was not even aware of the moment when Verna opened the car's door a few minutes later.

"I came to collect the plate," she called out gaily.

Receiving no answer, she now peered closely at the recumbent figure in the poor light.

"Are you asleep?" she whispered.

A soft snore was the only reply.

"Yes, you are, aren't you?"

He moved sideways restlessly and she darted back, not venturing closer until he had settled again.

Then she leaned closer.

"You are worn out."

A full moon shone through the window and by its beams she could see his face, relaxed in sleep.

How handsome he was, she thought.

She had been struck by his good looks in the first moment. Now she had the opportunity to examine him at leisure and they pleased her even more.

His face was lean, a high forehead and long straight nose. His mouth was wide and firm, revealing a hint of the humour that had so delighted her during the day. Beneath it his chin suggested stubbornness.

An intriguing combination she considered, smiling gently. Life with him could be very very interesting.

Then she checked herself, horrified at the way her thoughts were tending.

She knew nothing about him except that he was not a man of her own social standing.

And yet he was certainly a gentleman. His voice was cultured and he spoke with an instinctive authority that came from a lifetime of self-confidence. That was quite true despite his shabby clothes.

He was also beginning to show signs of a growth of dark beard, which gave him a slightly piratical look, she reflected, considering the matter with pleasure.

She leaned forward gently to look at him better and found that her mouth had come dangerously close to his.

She must back off at once.

But even while she was thinking this she found that she had crept a little nearer, so that her lips were brushing his.

Almost brushing his, she amended hastily.

Almost.

She had nearly kissed him, but not quite. Still, she must leave at once before she ran into danger.

She was still in time, she reassured herself as she hurried out of the door.

She had *nearly* kissed him, but she avoided it in time.

Yes, that was it.

She repeated it again and again as she ran back to the hotel. But she could still feel his lips against her own.

As she had feared, Winifred was waiting for her in their room, her hair in curlers, her face full of indignation.

"And just where do you think you have been?" she demanded in high dudgeon.

"I have been to visit the garage, enquiring after Mr. Payne's welfare," Verna answered with as much dignity as she could muster.

"The garage? Have you no sense of propriety?"

"Yes, far too much to accept his kindness without at least making certain that he is as comfortable as can be managed. It's horrid out there, all cold and dirty."

"It's probably what he's used to."

"No it is not. Do be fair, Winnie. You pretend to believe that he's a servant, but you must be able to see that he isn't."

"I see nothing of the kind and please don't call me Winnie."

"I quite often call you Winnie," Verna parried in a wheedling tone. "You've never minded before."

"You do it when you want something and you are not getting around me, my girl."

Verna merely gave a happy laugh.

Despite Winifred's caustic words she knew that her old friend loved her devotedly. Her mother had died many years before and Winifred was the nearest to a mother she had ever known.

"It's time you were in bed," she declared. "Now, keep still while I undress you."

But Verna, as was usual, was already removing her clothes without waiting for help.

"You should not do that. A great lady should stand still while her maid takes off her things."

"You'll never make a great lady of me, Winnie. I like doing things for myself."

"You do far too much for yourself. You should be statuesque and lofty."

"Heaven forbid. There's no fun in that!"

"Listen to me. You are not supposed to have fun. You are supposed to behave properly."

"I *hate* behaving properly."

"You don't need to tell me that. I've been trying to teach you propriety since you were a little girl and I have not succeeded yet."

"And you won't! I am not going to do the proper thing if it only means marrying some dreary creature just because he has a title."

"Much better than marrying a servant," Winifred came back darkly.

"He is *not* a servant."

"You don't know that. He could be anybody."

'Not just *anybody*,' Verna murmured to herself.

By now she had discarded her clothes and Winifred had slipped a blue nightgown over her head. Absorbed in her thoughts she sat docilely before the mirror.

She could see him now, lying fast asleep in the car – after his cheerful confidence of the day it had touched her to see him looking vulnerable, almost defenceless.

How tempting it had been to lean towards him and to study his shapely mouth that any woman would wish to kiss.

Not that she had actually kissed his lips she assured herself hastily – she had only thought about it.

But the feel of his lips against hers called her a liar. Her mouth had touched his, just briefly and the memory would haunt her until –

Until – ?

Until she could do the same again.

There! She had admitted it to herself.

From behind her she heard Winifred mumble,

"You'll realise that I'm right."

"I beg your pardon," she enquired, coming out of her reverie. "What did you say, Winifred?"

"If you ever listened to a word I say, which you *never* do – "

"I am listening to you now, I promise. What were you saying?"

"I've forgotten. Oh, yes – you'll find out that he's an upstart who's learned fine manners from the men he's worked for. That is, if you can call his manners fine."

"Obviously you don't."

"It wouldn't surprise me to learn that he's on the run from the law."

"Oh, Winnie, don't be so critical. Why on earth would you think that?"

"Because of the way he has to travel home. What kind of man has to seize an opportunity like this?"

"A very kind one."

"Or a convict. Or a servant who's just been thrown out of his employment without a reference."

"No, I think perhaps he is a younger son."

"Then he's a younger son without any money. Just look at him."

A smile crept over Verna's face. She was happy to look at him.

"Just what are you thinking?" Winifred demanded suspiciously.

"I'm considering his appearance as you suggested."

"Then consider his suit that needs a lot of attention from a valet and plainly hasn't had any. Then consider that he has no money – not even a younger son's allowance."

She sniffed as she came to her parting shot.

"In fact, it wouldn't surprise me to learn that this young man had sneaked out of his hotel without paying his bill!"

Then sublimely unaware of scoring a spectacular bullseye, Winifred climbed into bed and pulled the covers over her head.

CHAPTER FOUR

Michael fell asleep almost as soon as he had tucked himself in on the back seat of the car.

He was much more tired than he had imagined and slept without moving until, with a jerk, he woke up to find the light streaming in through the windows.

His watch told him it was seven-thirty.

He felt stiff all over, but managed to climb out of the car. At the far end of the building was a large sink with a tap, and here he managed to have some kind of a wash and make himself reasonably presentable.

A pageboy from the hotel came into the garage and spoke to him.

"Her Ladyship's compliments, monsieur, and will you please join her in the dining room?"

He had done his best with his appearance but, even so, he guessed he did not look like a suitable companion to join Lady Verna at breakfast. Winifred's withering glance would tell him so if he had any doubts.

Verna smiled, indicating the place beside her.

"You must eat a big breakfast. There is such a busy day ahead that you must keep your strength up."

The food was delicious and he ate willingly.

In half an hour they were on the road to Abbeville and from there to Etaples.

Michael drove fast and it was clear they were going to cover the distance in very good time.

Now they could see the sea and every moment they were growing closer to Calais.

"I wonder if we will catch a ferry tonight," Verna mused. "One thing I discovered on the way over here is that not all the boats take cars."

"I suppose there just aren't enough cars travelling to make the special arrangements worthwhile."

"That is just what I was told. I came over on the *Princess Charlotte*, and if we are lucky we can catch the same boat back to Dover."

In the event their luck held.

As they drove into the harbour at Calais they could already see the *Princess Charlotte* waiting on the quay.

"We'll have to hurry," Verna said, reaching into her bag for her purse. "Can you drive me to the booking office and I will buy the tickets."

"I cannot take the car beyond this barrier," Michael replied. "I'll come with you. You mustn't go through that crowd alone."

He wondered if he should suggest leaving her here while he went to buy the tickets, but that would mean her giving him the money, which he would find awkward.

While he was pondering which course to take, she seized his hand and hurried off, calling, "we'll be back in a moment," over her shoulder at Winifred.

When they reached the ticket office and he could see how much money was involved in the passage for three people and a car, Michael was glad that he had not let her give it to him.

He swore that never again would he find himself in this situation.

From now on he would lead a reformed life – sober, respectable and above all honourable. And he would never allow himself to run short of money.

But then looking at the delightful Verna, he realised that he was only repeating a vow he had made ever since he met her.

Was that really only recently?

It seemed like a lifetime.

"You are just in time for the crossing, monsieur," the clerk informed him. "We have one other car travelling tonight and the ramp is still down."

"I wish to stay by the car all the time," he insisted.

"Not possible, monsieur. You must leave it with the attendants, but you may go to see it later."

A door was opened in the side of the ship, through which a ramp had been eased down onto the quay.

Up this ramp a motor car was being pulled by two men and pushed by another four.

As they watched, it reached the top of the ramp and vanished into the body of the ship. They hurried to where they had left the car under Winifred's stern protection.

They reached it to find an incredible sight.

The lovely vehicle had attracted much attention and was now surrounded by eager boys, who walked around it admiringly and some ventured to touch it.

Winifred took great exception to them and used her umbrella vigorously on their hands, shouting,

"Be off!"

They vanished.

"I do apologise for leaving you alone with the car," volunteered Michael. "I should have known better."

But Winifred was not to be placated.

"You need not think that I needed your help," she declared proudly. "I'm quite capable of using an umbrella to good effect!"

Her eyes kindled as she added,

"On *anyone.*"

"I am sure you are," admitted Michael. "It looked very painful. "But we're here now and I must take the car to the ramp while you ladies prepare to board."

"We are quite aware of that, young man," Winifred said loftily. "We have done this before – on the way out."

"Yes, ma'am," he responded meekly.

As he jumped behind the wheel Winifred climbed out. It took just a moment to swing round and head for the ramp where the attendants were waiting for him.

Reluctantly he handed the vehicle over to them and walked back to where he had left the ladies. Together they headed for the point where passengers embarked and soon they were on board the great ship.

"It will be leaving very soon," exclaimed Verna.

Winifred gave a faint groan.

"Yes dear, I've remembered how seasick you get," Verna told her. "That's why I have booked a cabin just for you. We'll find it now and you can lie down."

"And you must stay with me," insisted Winifred.

"No, I'll leave you to rest," Verna parried quickly.

"Can I give you my arm to your cabin?" Michael asked Winifred.

"Thank you, I can manage, if my Lady will come with me," Winifred snorted in high dudgeon.

"Yes, ma'am."

"There is no necessity for you to come with us," she added as he began to follow them.

"I'll wait for her Ladyship on deck."

As he walked away he allowed himself a quiet grin.

Winifred's hostility was rather amusing and he was enjoying anticipation of the moment when she learned his true identity.

For half-an-hour he stood on the deck, watching the crew making preparations to depart. At last the ship gave a small lurch and they began to move away from the quay.

He was wondering if Verna would be able to join him after all. He was sure that Winifred would keep her in the cabin if she could.

"There you are," called a voice from behind him.

He turned and there was Verna smiling at him.

"Did you think I wasn't coming?" she enquired.

"I was afraid of it. Winifred has now really taken against me, despite my efforts to defer to her."

Verna chuckled and tucked her hand in his arm.

"Yes, I saw you trying to be meek."

"I'm not usually meek," he agreed wryly.

"And you don't find it easy – "

"No, but not much longer now, thank goodness."

"Oh!" she looked offended. "Are you so eager to be rid of me?"

"No, I didn't mean that," he apologised hastily.

She laughed and in the fast fading light he could see a gleam in her eyes. She was enjoying teasing him.

Suddenly he was disconcerted and could not think of what to say.

"I think – " he began.

"Yes?"

"I think – "

He still could not find the words.

"You think what?"

"I think – perhaps we should go below to see the car. I am a little concerned lest people try to steal from it."

"Can people really be so greedy?"

"I am afraid people are greedy in every walk of life. It does not matter if it is a car, a bicycle or something you have sent for repair, you have to be careful it is not taken from you. I remember my father – "

He stopped, cursing himself for carelessness. He had been about to say that his father once had some fine pictures stolen, forgetting he was supposed to be a pauper.

"What about your father?" she questioned.

"Oh – nothing really. Somebody picked his pocket. It can happen at any time."

"Tell me about your father."

"There's nothing much to tell – ah, there's the car. It seems to be all right, but we had better go and sit in it."

He handed her in and climbed inside beside her.

"We need to discuss what we are going to do when we land. Where do you want me to drive you?"

"But how can I ask you to drive me any further?"

"Will anyone be meeting you?"

"No. Nobody knows that I am coming home. But I drove myself to Dover before and I can manage again."

"I don't think that would be a good idea," he said firmly. "Where will you go?"

"To my home in the country."

"However well you managed on the way out, you must not try to do so again."

"*Must* not?" she asked him.

He had briefly forgotten that, while she considered him a servant, he was in no position to tell her what to do.

He took a deep breath.

"Must not," he repeated. "You have placed your safety in my hands and must take my advice. I will escort you to your home in Kent."

"How do you know I live in Kent?"

"I have heard of Challoner Abbey," he said quickly. "It's not too far from my own home."

It was quite a relief to know that he could drive her home, then proceed to Belmont Park and assume his title.

He wondered if he should now tell her the full truth about his identity. But he was reluctant to do so, in case the knowledge of his title made her more interested in him.

He tried to tell himself that this wonderful girl was above such tiresome considerations yet caution was deeply ingrained in him.

He had been run after by a great number of women, some of whom he found fascinating for a short time.

They were attractive and he had made love to them, but inevitably after a brief while he had been disappointed by them.

He kept telling himself time after time that he was being ridiculous and asking too much. But in his heart he knew that they were attracted to his title and the woman he did marry must love him for himself alone.

'What I need is love,' he had told himself over and over again, 'from a woman who loves me for myself and myself only.'

Now, for the first time, he was with a wonderful girl who had simply no idea of his worldly position. Yet she seemed to enjoy his company, actually seemed happy with him.

And he wanted this glorious time to last forever.

"I just cannot let you drive me such a distance," she said. "I am sure you have affairs of your own to see to."

"Do you really think that when we reach England I could merely shake you by the hand, say goodbye and then walk away?"

As he spoke he took her hand in his, as if to shake it. Actually he just sat still holding it and wondering if she had squeezed his hand back or it was just his wishful thinking.

"No," she murmured softly. "I don't think that."

"Will you miss me when finally we say goodbye to each other?"

"Of course I will," Verna answered him. "You have been so marvellous in every way."

She paused for a moment before she questioned,

"Shall we ever see each other again?"

He could hardly hear the words. They were almost said in a whisper.

"We must – "

There was a short silence before Verna whispered,

"Do you really want to see me again?"

"I would like to see you very much," he replied. "The moment I saw you I thought you were different from anyone I had ever seen before. Now I find it is *impossible* to say goodbye."

There was more silence before she muttered,

"I want – more than I can possibly say – to go on seeing you."

"That is what I want, too. So – "

Suddenly he knew what he had to do. It was sheer madness, but it was magnificent.

"You will probably laugh at me," he stated baldly, "but *I want to marry you*."

For a moment neither of them moved.

Then Verna tightened her fingers on his. He gave an answering squeeze, but he did not speak.

She was looking at him with wonder.

"Do you really mean it? We have only just met."

Michael could barely speak.

Then, as he felt her tremble, he sighed,

"I knew the moment I saw you, you were so unlike any woman I had met before. There was something about you which made me feel I could not lose you."

He smiled at her as he continued,

"I want you, Verna, I want you more than I have ever wanted any woman in the whole of my life. It seems impossible I should feel like this when we've only known each other for such a short time. But I know that if I lose you now, I will never be happy again."

Verna drew in her breath.

Then she answered him in a low fervent voice,

"And I love you too. It might seem strange, but I realised the moment I saw you that you also were different from anyone I had ever known. Now I know that it was because I was falling in love."

"That's exactly what I feel," he cried joyfully. "So, my darling, we'll be married as soon as we can arrange it."

Verna drew in her breath.

"Do you mean that. Do you really mean it?"

"Yes of course I mean it, Verna, I have been in love before – or thought I was. Yet there was always something missing which told me that what I felt was more to do with my imagination than reality."

His voice deepened as he continued,

"But with you everything is new. I know now that I must never let you go – "

"I don't want you to leave me," she sighed. "I want to stay with you. Do you really want me to be your wife?"

"With all my heart. There will be many difficulties, but we will both overcome them. You must be certain that you want me as much as I want you."

"But I do, *I do*."

"I love you! I love you! You must never doubt it, Verna."

"I never will. I just love you so much. I can hardly believe that you want me. But what did you mean about difficulties?"

"Well – "

"Oh, I understand," she said, breaking into a merry little laugh. "You mean because I have a silly title and you don't have one. But that doesn't matter. I am of age and can marry whom I please. Papa won't oppose me when he knows how much I am in love with you."

"Even if I have no money?" he asked, hardly able to believe his luck. "And that socially I'm just a nobody?"

"What matters is that you are *you*. Just love me, that is all I ask."

"With all my heart and for all my life," he vowed.

"Heaven seems to have opened for me and if you and I are together for the rest of our lives, it will be Heaven itself on earth."

Then he could contain himself no longer and seized her in his arms and kissed her.

She returned his kiss with fervour.

In the back of her mind Verna knew that this was not really how a well-brought-up young lady was supposed to behave. Winifred would faint if she knew.

But she cared about nothing, except that she was in

the arms of the man she loved and wished to stay there for ever.

When they finally drew apart, she was trembling and breathless.

"Oh, my love," she murmured.

When he did not reply, she looked anxiously into his face.

"What is it?" she asked.

"There's something I have to tell you, my dearest. I had meant to save it until later, but if you are so willing to entrust your life to me – "

"For ever and ever," she avowed.

"Then you must know the truth."

"Is the truth *so* very terrible? I just don't believe it. Everything about you is wonderful."

"Thank you. But I am not what I seem. I've been playing a part, because I had to. But when we reach home, I can become my own true self."

"Who is your true self?"

"I am the Earl of Belmont – at least, I will be when I reach home and assume the title. My father has just died. That is why I was hurrying home."

"The Earl of Belmont?" she repeated slowly. "Are you making fun of me?"

"I don't blame you for thinking so, darling. I don't look much like an Earl, do I? But believe me, it's true."

"But how – I mean – ?"

"Just how does an Earl come to look like a tramp, without enough money to get home? It's a long story and it does not do me much credit. I have lived selfishly, never thinking about anyone but myself.

"But all that will change, because of my great love

for you. I want you to know the truth that you will not be marrying a nobody."

"You could never be a nobody," she averred. "You are the man I adore and that makes you somebody."

"I'll be somebody when you have married me!"

"It cannot be too soon for me," Verna whispered, "and it will be wonderful to be married to you. It doesn't matter that you are an Earl, although, of course, I am very glad. I would love you if you were just '*Mr. Nobody*'.

"It is so marvellous finding you when I thought I would never find anyone so wonderful, so exciting and so handsome."

Michael smiled.

"Now you are flattering me and I love it. As long as you feel like that about me, I want you to go on telling me from first thing in the morning until last thing at night."

Verna laughed.

"How could I have known, how could I have ever guessed that I would find you? It is the most marvellous thing that has ever happened to me."

"I can say the same," Michael breathed. "I will be honest and tell you I have known a few beautiful women, but none has ever been as beautiful as you are or makes me feel as you make me feel and that because you are mine, I possess the most fabulous jewel in the whole world."

Verna gave a cry.

"Please go on thinking that way for always. I was certain that I would never fall in love with anyone."

"So you really are in love with me?"

"More than I can possibly tell you, even if we live for a thousand years," replied Verna.

Michael drew in his breath.

"I have something to tell you that may make you feel differently about me."

Verna looked up at him with surprised eyes.

He became aware that for the moment she found it impossible to breathe.

Then she said in a voice he could hardly hear,

"What have you to tell me?"

Now Michael found that he was nervous.

"It may shock you," he warned, "and you may feel that you cannot marry me after all."

"But why? Why do you say that? What have you done?"

"My father and I didn't always get on well together. He was a very rich man but, because he was annoyed with me, he cut off my allowance."

He paused to gather his courage,

"He told me that I should receive nothing from him when he died and the money and the family estate would all go to my younger brother.

"He could not deny me the title, but he could deny me his money. So, except for a small amount I inherited from my mother, I am more or less penniless!"

He thought as he was speaking, he was destroying his heart.

How could Verna love him after this news?

Then, in a very quiet voice, she replied,

"I love you, Michael, and you love me. Love is not determined by money. As long as we both love each other, I think we are the *richest* people on earth."

"Do you mean it? My darling, we might find life extremely difficult and have to count every penny before we spend it."

"I don't think money matters one way or another. Somehow God will look after us, because he has already given us the greatest gift of all."

"Do you really mean that?" he asked.

"I mean it because it is the real truth. I love you because you are you. I don't care if you are a millionaire or just plain Mr. Michael, as long as you are *you*."

With a gasp of joy he drew her even closer to him, her head against his shoulder.

He looked down at her, his lips seeking hers.

Then he was kissing her again – kissing her wildly, passionately until he could feel her sublime body quivering against his.

She clung to him fiercely, feeling that they had both reached Heaven.

They were united by their shared love.

What could possibly go wrong now?

CHAPTER FIVE

Michael felt that he could sit there forever with his beloved Verna in his arms. He had never in his life felt so happy as he was at this very moment.

If only he could find a way to make their happiness last.

But he recognised that, for this to happen, he must be completely honest with her.

"I still haven't told you the whole story. I told you that my father cut me off, but I did not explain how much of it was my own fault. I said I lived selfishly, but it was more than that. I have been self-indulgent, thoughtless – "

"Hush!" She stopped him with her fingers over his mouth. "That was the *old* you. The new you starts right now and he is the man I know and love."

"Bless you. But I must take action to make certain that the past really *is* the past. For instance – "

"Go on," Verna teased him when he hesitated.

"I gambled all my money away and when I heard about my father's death, I just did not have enough to get back to England."

"So that is why you needed to come with me!"

"Yes, but there is worse to come. The reason you see me in these clothes is that I had to pawn my best ones. Even so, I was still short of money, so I – "

He gulped.

"You what?" Verna asked anxiously.

"I left my hotel without paying the bill," he forced himself to say.

Eyes wide, she stared at him.

"You did what?" she demanded very slowly.

Michael heartily wished that he had not started to tell her this story. He could tell from her face that she was shocked and disbelieving.

"I escaped without paying my bill, but of course I'll send them the money as soon as I can. Verna please don't condemn me – "

He was interrupted by the last sound he expected to hear. Verna leaned back against the seat as peal after peal of laughter burst from her.

"My darling," he stuttered, half in delight and half in disbelief, "I am glad that you can see the funny side – "

"Oh, but you don't know," she choked. "It's much funnier than you can imagine. Oh dear, oh dear – "

She went off in another burst of laughter, clutching her side, rocking back and forth.

"I am so sorry," she gasped at last. "It's just that – Winifred – "

"Winifred?" he cried in alarm. "For Heaven's sake, don't tell her. She thinks badly enough of me already."

"She thinks you look just like the sort of man who would sneak out of a hotel without paying his bill," Verna chuckled. "She said so last night."

"She said what?" asked Michael, aghast. "What a terrible thing to say about me. I call that impertinent."

"I call it accurate," she laughed, managing to calm down. "After all, it's exactly what you did."

"Yes, but – " he subsided, laughing reluctantly.

"Just promise me that you'll never tell her. I would never live it down."

"Ah, but wait until she learns who you really are."

"It might be better for her not to know for a while, Verna, let's keep it to ourselves until we get home."

"Perhaps your father did not cut you off without a penny after all," she mused. "I didn't like him, but I can't believe him capable of that."

Michael stared.

"You knew my father?"

"Not 'knew' exactly, but I did meet him a couple of times. He and my father quarrelled years ago over a piece of land they both wanted to buy, I think. So years passed without any meetings.

"Then they bumped into each other at some party. They didn't exactly become friends, but they seem to have been bored with being enemies. I've met your sister Jane and your brother Anthony, but you were never there."

"I was most probably spending my life abroad by that time. So that's how we have lived so close, yet missed meeting each other all these years."

She squeezed his hand.

"We have a lot of time to make up for."

He leaned down and kissed her tenderly.

"The ship is slowing down," she sighed. "We will be landing in a minute. I had better go and find Winifred."

"I'll wait for you on deck, my darling."

As they emerged into fresh air, the dawn was just breaking and they could see the port of Dover just ahead.

Verna went below deck and returned with Winifred a few minutes later.

Michael enquired very politely after her health and

received a frosty reply. It was clear that Winifred was in an unyielding mood and he doubted that she would warm to him any more when she learned the truth.

To his relief she fell asleep in the back seat as soon as they were on the road. After a few miles he could hear her snoring gently just behind them, so he asked Verna,

"What sort of wedding shall we have? A big grand ceremony in London or something in the country?"

"I would like to marry you quietly without any fuss and commotion. People asked to weddings always have so much to say and those not asked are furious. So let us be married in your village Church with no one present except your close relations."

"What about your relations?"

Verna laughed.

"Most of my relations are annoyed with me because I would not marry the man they had chosen. I was always afraid that if I weakened, I would wake up and find myself wife to a stranger.

"I knew I could never fall in love with any of those men my family had chosen for me. But as soon as I saw you, I knew that you were so unlike all the others."

"That's just what I feel about you. So, my darling, there is no reason why we should not be blissfully happy for ever. There may be difficulties – one especially, but we will fight all our troubles together."

The words came from the very depths of his heart.

She moved a little closer to him and put her hand on his knee.

"I love you! I love you, my Michael, I am so happy that I would like to go on driving with you until Eternity. Then we would never have to be worried by other people."

"If we remain as much in love as we are now, then

we are strong enough to take on the world. I will be yours as you will be mine until, please God, we will both go to Heaven together."

"How lovely – " she sighed.

They drove on, sometimes talking to each other and sometimes just continuing to feel they were close together.

Now that Michael was in a more cheerful mood, he wondered if perhaps he was being too gloomy. His father might not yet have changed his will, and even if he had, he would probably not cut his heir off without a single penny.

It was likely that he would receive at least a small inheritance, one that would be enough to live on with the addition of his mother's legacy.

Failing that his brother might be generous and spare him something of what their father had left him.

As if she had followed his thoughts, Verna cried,

"Everything is going to be all right. I just know it."

"I'm sure of it too, unless – " suddenly he was riven with doubts again.

"Unless what?"

"Unless your family forbids you to marry me. I suppose I could hardly blame them."

"They cannot. I am twenty-five and my money is my own. Nobody can stop me doing anything I want."

"Nobody?"

"Nobody at all. Not even a husband – "

She chuckled.

"You will find that out, sir, after we are married."

"As long as you are my wife, I shall never object to anything you do."

"Oh, what a rash promise," she exclaimed merrily. "I shall certainly remind you of it one day, when we have been married a very long time and you say, 'my wife is not going to do *that*'."

"Just as long as I can say the beautiful words, 'my wife'," Michael sighed happily.

"No matter what happens, Michael, you know I will come with you. If we had to walk barefoot to India, we would go there together!"

"But I don't want to see you barefoot, my darling. I want you to have the best of everything."

"If I have you," she added contentedly, "I have the best of everything. Oh, I cannot wait to get home. Can't you drive a little faster?"

"You think your father would have a better opinion of me if I too had a conviction for speeding?"

"As a matter of fact, he probably would! Also, I have heard he was a bit of a rip when he was young. You two will have a lot in common. All will be well."

Michael wished he could share her confidence. But he knew from the experiences of his friends that a father who had kicked up wild larks in his youth was likely to be harder – not easier – on his daughter's suitor.

'I know what he got up to,' Michael recalled one of them saying. 'I know because I got up to it myself and I'm dashed if my girl is marrying anyone like me.'

But he tried to stay optimistic and after a while he said,

"I don't think that I should come to your house. It would be better for me to go to my own home and find out what the position is and what I have to offer you. I believe that my inheritance may be limited and I must know how much I have before I can face your father."

"But it really doesn't matter," she replied ardently. "You'll still be the Earl, and that's all that my father will see. If a wealthy tradesman offered for my hand, he would ignore the money and see only the lack of title. No, you must come back with me now. I insist."

When he did not reply, she took his arm.

"I don't want to let you out of my sight, in case you vanish forever."

"I will never do so. You are wonderful, adorable, in fact everything I have ever longed for. I will be yours as you will be mine until the end of Eternity."

Verna gave a cry.

"You say such wonderful things. How is it possible I have been able to find you?"

Michael gave a laugh.

"I thought I had found *you*."

"We found each other," replied Verna. "Promise we will go on loving each other. Whatever your family says or whatever the problems are that lay ahead, they must not matter because we have each other."

"That is just what I was going to say to you. We will be married whatever anyone says, does or thinks. *They* are not important. The only important one is *you*."

He thought the happiness they were feeling seemed to turn the world into a perfect place and it would be quite impossible to be worried about anything.

They drove on and soon they found a country hotel where they could stop for lunch.

As they climbed out of the car Michael realised that Winifred was fast asleep in the back. He woke her gently, and she glared at him – she had been enjoying her sleep.

If only, he thought, they could leave her asleep and quietly creep away together, but his conscience would not let him do it. So he told her they were going in for lunch, and helped her down.

Then unexpectedly, she solved his problem for him, complaining loudly about being disturbed, so that Verna had an inspiration and hired a room for her.

"You can finish your sleep there, Winnie dear," she cooed.

So she and Michael had a pleasant lunch together in an empty dining room, so there was no one to hear all their loving words as they sat by the window, looking out at the flowers in the garden.

"This has been wonderful," Verna enthused as they sipped their coffee. "I feel somehow that we are part of the flowers and everything is going to be as beautiful for us as they are – "

"You must not expect too much," Michael told her. "As long as we have each other, nothing else matters."

"That is what I was trying to say. Oh, Michael I do love you and every moment I am with you, I love you so much more."

"Verna, you are the only one who matters in the whole world. If your family tries to take you away from me, I'll fight them, because I cannot and will not lose you."

"You will never lose me. I am so blissfully happy now I that have found you and I promise we will never lose each other until we die."

They left in a cloud of happy harmony, which soon vanished in comical suddenness when Verna declared her intention of driving the car the rest of the way.

"I cannot let you do so," Michael declared flatly.

"May I please remind you, sir, that I drove to Dover without male assistance," she countered with a deft touch of haughtiness. "I can easily manage the short drive ahead of us."

"That may have been all very well at one time," he started to say, "but now that we are engaged – "

Then he stopped.

Verna was looking at him impishly.

"I told you that you would start trying to order me about, but I did think that you would wait until we were actually married!"

"I am only concerned for your safety."

"I shall be perfectly safe."

To forestall any further argument she leapt into the driving seat, leaving him no choice but to climb up beside her. He just made it before the car started to move.

They bickered amiably for a couple of miles before she suddenly terrified him by swinging the car violently to the right and heading back the way they had come.

"What are you doing?" he yelled.

"*Going back for Winifred*!"

After that he was silent.

*

Two hours later with Michael driving the car this time, they reached Verna's home and turned into a pair of huge elaborate gates.

The drive was impressive and so was the house – it was large and ancient, and it had clearly had a lot of money spent on it over the years.

In fact it looked bigger and more prosperous than the house that he himself had been raised in. The garden was bright with flowers and obviously well-kept.

As he drew up outside, an important-looking butler opened the front door and Verna exclaimed,

"We have done it!"

As they entered the house, servants appeared. She told them to take their luggage from the back of the car and went to speak to the butler, whilst Michael returned to the car to supervise the unloading.

He offered Winifred his arms to help her descend, but received a thunderous look that made him back off.

Instead she accepted the butler's arm, declaring that only in this way could she feel *safe*.

The word 'safe' had been more than prominent in her conversation ever since they had collected her from the hotel where she had been sitting, awaiting their return in a black fury.

Michael had no doubt that in Winifred's mind it was all his fault!

Once Winifred had swept grandly into the house, he rejoined Verna in the hall and she informed him,

"I have told the butler you will be staying here and which room I want you to have."

She slipped her arm into his and drew him further inside, giving him a chance to admire the lofty hall.

She took him into a large room that opened off the hall and he guessed it must have been a banqueting room at some time in the past.

There was an attractive young woman sitting at one of the windows and she rose as they entered.

Verna kissed her saying,

"Mary dear, you may be surprised to see me, but I have so much to tell you, as so many exciting things have happened. But first of all, let me introduce Lord Belmont who has been kind enough to drive me home. Michael – this is my sister, Mary."

Mary's eyes flickered over Michael, making him wish he had stuck to his resolution to go home and change first. Obviously she was surprised at hearing who he was.

She held out her hand and asked,

"Have you really brought Verna home? We were all a little concerned when she set off like that with only Winifred for company, but she's always been headstrong."

"Thank you very much," muttered Verna, accepting it as a compliment.

She smiled as she continued,

"I suppose it was really my fault for arriving at Andrew's home without warning, but he was on the verge of going to Italy and didn't want to be bothered with me."

She gave a crow of laughter.

"All he could think of was courting a rich bride."

"The way he spends money he needs a rich bride," remarked Mary. "But he should have taken you with him, not left you to return to England alone."

"Well, it all worked out for the best," said Verna. "My friend here has been kind enough to drive for me and, as he will be staying the night, after what has been quite an exhausting journey, we must make him very comfortable."

She looked adoringly at Michael as she spoke.

He was aware that her sister was staring at them both with some astonishment.

Then Mary held out her hand to Michael,

"Thank you for looking after my sister. It is most kind of you to have driven her home. I hope you will be comfortable with us tonight. Now I am sure you would like something to drink."

A footman came in carrying a drinks tray.

"I am extremely thirsty," sighed Verna. "I am sure Michael is too after driving so far."

While they were having their drinks, Verna's sister left the room, saying she must see to some arrangements.

Verna moved closer to Michael,

"Mary is my eldest sister and the most important one. Now Mama is dead, she gives the orders and more or less runs everything in the house."

"I will be on my best behaviour," Michael promised and they both laughed.

"Now that Mama is dead we often find Papa very difficult. The best thing is to agree with him in everything he says."

"I will do my best. All the same, my darling, I am a little nervous that your family will not be impressed by me as things are at the moment."

"Don't tell them everything immediately. Let them find out for themselves about your situation."

There was silence before Michael reflected,

"I *do* believe that we should be truthful. Whilst you love me despite everything, your family will most probably feel differently. We will have to convince them."

"And we will," she asserted. "We must."

Verna threw herself into his arms and he embraced her. But even as they kissed the door opened and a man came in.

He was grey-haired and dignified with an upright bearing and something told Michael that this was Verna's father.

He was a good-looking man and must have been exceedingly striking when he was young. But now his face was hard, his manner haughty and there was an expression in his eyes which Michael thought was rather frightening.

He walked quickly towards Michael,

"I understand that you have just driven my daughter back from France in the new car. I am very grateful to you for doing so."

Michael shook him by the hand and replied,

"It was a great pleasure, sir. I think she would have found it difficult if she had to drive herself."

"Mary has told me what happened. I think it was disgraceful of my son to abandon her – even allowing for the inconsiderate ways of brothers."

"I agree, sir."

"So, I am very grateful to you. I understand we are to have the pleasure of your company tonight and that is excellent. But first, let us introduce ourselves. You have doubtless learnt that I am Lord Challoner, but I have not yet been told your name."

For a moment Michael hesitated before replying,

"I was told just before I left France that my father had died. That means I have to take his place as head of my family. He was the Earl of Belmont."

There was a long pause, during which Michael felt the air chill several degrees.

"Your father – Belmont?" Lord Challoner asked in a disbelieving voice.

"Yes, sir."

"And you are the new *Earl*?"

"I know I don't look like one, but I've had several accidents recently," Michael hastened to say. "I really am Lord Belmont."

"Hmm, I heard a rumour that your father was dead, and that the family was keeping it a secret for a while."

"That was to give me time to come home."

He felt Verna's hand touch his and realised that he must bring matters to a head at once.

"Verna and I have a matter that we would wish to discuss with you, sir."

Lord Challoner looked at Michael in some surprise at hearing this stranger use his daughter's first name.

"It's important, Papa," added Verna.

"Then we had better go into the smoking room."

He walked out of the room and they followed.

Something told Michael that Verna was worried.

He led them across the hall and along a corridor to the smoking room, a large room with sofas and armchairs in front of an attractive fireplace with a huge fire burning.

Lord Challoner sat down on one of the chairs while Verna chose the sofa – and because she obviously wanted him to, Michael sat beside her.

For a moment no one spoke.

Then as if Lord Challoner had already guessed why they wanted to speak to him, he urged them,

"Now come along. Tell me what you want me to know, although I have an idea what it is."

Michael smiled.

"As I told you my father is now dead," he began, "and I must return to my home tomorrow. But, sir, before I leave, I request your permission to marry your daughter."

He took a deep breath before he went on,

"We have not known each other for very long, but we have both fallen deeply in love. Despite the fact I am in mourning, I wish to marry Verna as soon as possible!"

There was a long silence.

Lord Challoner's demeanour remained impassive and he seemed almost frightening. Verna jumped up from the sofa and went to her father's side.

She knelt down putting her arms round him.

"We are very happy Papa, and I want, as Michael wishes, to be married as soon as possible!"

"I can see no reason why you should be in such a hurry," her father responded slowly.

"We want to be together, Papa, we are in love and we want to be married quietly and without any fuss."

There was a long and uncomfortable pause before he replied,

"I would like to know a little more about you, Lord Belmont, than I do at the moment. In fact if your father has only just died, there is much explaining for you to do."

Almost as if he forced himself to speak, Michael asserted fervently,

"I have loved Verna ever since I met her. That was only a short time ago, but we knew at once that we were meant for each other. I have thus come to see you instead of going, as I should have done, back to my own home.

"But I must be honest and tell you that before I left England to go to France, my father told me that whilst he could not prevent me from inheriting the Belmont title, he was leaving all his money to my younger brother."

As he finished speaking, the Earl looked at him in astonishment while Verna cried out,

"How cruel! I have never heard of anyone behaving like that before."

"Nor have I," agreed Lord Challoner, "so it makes things very difficult."

"It makes no difference to me," Verna countered stubbornly.

"I am afraid that it does, my dear Verna. I consider the situation a serious one. It is something we will need to discuss very carefully before I can give you permission to marry my daughter.

"In the meantime I forbid you to regard yourselves as engaged!"

CHAPTER SIX

When Lord Challoner had finished speaking he rose to his feet.

"I think this is something we should talk over after you have rested," he announced, his manner chilly.

He paused a moment and then added,

"I suggest, Verna, that you now go and change your clothes and perhaps have a hot bath. Then you and I will sit down and discuss the matter together later on today."

Before Michael could say anything, he had turned and walked from the room.

For a moment both Michael and Verna were silent.

Then Verna gave a little gasp,

"Papa is going to be difficult, I know he is going to be difficult! But promise you will go on loving me."

"For ever," he vowed. "If the worst comes to the worst we will run away and get married in the first Church we come to."

He smiled at her as he added,

"And I can work. I will find something to do which will, if nothing else, provide us with enough money to be reasonably comfortable."

Verna threw her arms around his neck.

"Even if Papa is difficult, as long as we are together and you love me and I love you, nothing else matters!"

"All the same, my darling, we have to live, we have

to eat and we have to have somewhere to sleep. It is going to be very hard."

"I will do anything to stay with you," Verna cried, "even work as a servant."

Michael kissed her tenderly and then as he felt her quiver against him, he carried on kissing her.

A little later he raised his head to say,

"I think, darling, I should go to my room and try to make myself look respectable."

'*How*?' asked a little voice in his brain. 'You have one suitcase with some underclothes and nothing else.'

When he had gone Verna put her hands to her eyes.

'I love him! I love him!' she told herself.

Then because she was beginning to feel frightened of what might happen, she prayed to God to help them, so that they could always be together.

It was a prayer from the very depths of her soul.

Then she walked across to the window and looking over the garden she thought how beautiful it was with all the flowers in bloom.

'I adore my home,' she thought to herself. 'I love being here, but if I have to live without a garden in a house which is so small we can hardly move, as long as I am with Michael, that is all I care for.'

At the same time she was scared.

She knew how intimidating her father could be with anything that concerned her and her sisters.

She could only pray that, even if it took a miracle, he would understand how much Michael meant to her and how much she meant to him.

But for now she had something important that must be done, so she hurried up the stairs to Winifred's room to find her already unpacking.

"Winifred dear," Verna began hurriedly, "I want to talk to you."

Winifred sniffed.

"About *him,* I suppose."

"Yes, him. About Lord Belmont, my true love and the man I intend to marry. No, don't look at me like that. I am not mad. Old Lord Belmont is dead and Michael, his elder son, has come home to assume the title."

"That creature? He has spun you a story and you believe it!"

"It's the truth," said Verna seriously. "He has told me everything, including about the troubles in his family. But I love him and nothing is going to come between us."

"Your Papa will have something to say about it."

But Verna resolved that she would not be deterred.

She loved Michael and knew that he loved her and she would not allow herself to be afraid of anything while she knew that his heart was hers.

"I know it will not be easy to persuade Papa, but he simply must say yes, because if he doesn't, my heart will break. Oh, Winnie dear, you won't say anything against my darling, will you?"

"Hmm!"

"Promise me," Verna pleaded.

"What can I say *for* him? That we picked him up as a vagabond, hiring himself out – "

Verna gave a little scream.

"No, no, nothing like that. Just stay very quiet and agree with everything I say."

"I'll try."

"You wouldn't want to see me heart-broken, would you?"

"But why *him*?" wailed Winifred. "Why couldn't you choose one of those respectable young men who have wanted to marry you?"

"Because not one of them was '*the one*'. None of them smiles like him or can make me laugh. None of them makes my heart beat so hard – just by looking at me."

"But that's a whole lot of romantic fiddle-faddle!" protested Winifred. "What matters is position in Society, a secure life, enough money to live on without fear – "

But Verna was shaking her head.

"No, they do *not* matter. What really matters is a man who loves you as much as you love him, knowing that you are sheltered in his arms and in his heart – that he is yours forever and ever, just as you are his."

"And suppose nobody in Society will ever speak to you again?"

"As long as *he* speaks to me, I will not care. As long as *he* kisses me, so that I melt inside with love for him – oh, Winnie, have you never been kissed like that?"

To her surprise a sadness settled over her face.

"Yes," she admitted at last. "But he died."

"Oh, darling."

Overcome with pity, Verna threw her arms around Winifred.

"It's all right," Winifred added gruffly. "It was a long time ago. I'll do whatever you want. And I only hope that you will be luckier."

"I will," vowed Verna. "I am definitely going to be the happiest woman on earth!"

*

Upstairs Michael found himself taken into a huge magnificent bed chamber with a four-poster bed.

Its opulence was overwhelming and he wondered if that was the whole point.

This view was confirmed by Rogers, the valet who had been assigned to him, and who confided that he had originally been given a smaller room on the next floor. But the orders had been changed at the last minute.

"They've realised that you're more important than they thought, my Lord," was his explanation.

He might be right, Michael thought.

Possibly this was the courtesy thought proper for a man who aspired to a daughter of the house, especially if he held the title of Earl.

Or perhaps Lord Challoner was simply making it plain that he was being presumptuous in even thinking of Verna?

The problem of his clothes was solved for him in an unexpected way by Maureen. She was Lord Challoner's second daughter and she had displeased him by marrying against his wishes and after three years her husband had died, prompting her father to remark that he had always predicted it would end badly.

A tearful Lady Maureen had then been persuaded to return home, bringing her late husband's clothes with her, all she had left of him.

She now lived in permanent mourning, but she was a kind-hearted soul and, when Verna appealed to her, had no hesitation in loaning out the evening clothes that had belonged to 'dear Henry'.

"But it will make Lord Challoner think even worse of me," Michael commented doubtfully.

"But how should he know?" Lady Maureen asked. "Men in formal evening attire all look exactly the same!"

He thanked her and accepted her generous offer.

To his relief the suit fitted him perfectly and when he looked in the glass he really seemed quite respectable.

He began to wish that he had concealed his worries from Verna's father until he discovered the worst.

After all, when he did reach home, things might not be so bad.

There was a gentle knock on the door and Verna stood there, looking glorious in a blue satin dress. About her neck was a grand necklace of diamonds and sapphires.

"Papa told me to wear it," she confided. "He said that you must be shown every courtesy."

"It's beautiful, Verna."

At the back of his mind was the suspicion that Lord Challoner wanted to display his daughter's wealth to make a point to her possibly impoverished suitor.

"I want you to meet the rest of the family before Papa joins us," continued Verna. "They are all gathered downstairs to meet you."

She explained that she had three sisters, Mary and Maureen, who he had already met, and Phoebe, who was nineteen.

"Papa is the most devoted father in the world," she said. "In fact, he finds it hard to part with any of us. We all have our own income, so he cannot actually prevent us, but he can make it very difficult."

"I am completely astonished that he allowed you to drive to France," observed Michael.

"Ah, it's because I appealed to his one weakness."

"I am astonished to discover he has any weakness!"

"It's his love of motoring and his pride in me as a driver. It overcomes all his prejudices against independent females. Even so he nearly gave way at the last minute.

When I was sitting in the car, the engine running, he began to say, 'on second thoughts I wonder if you – '

"But I shall never discover what he was wondering. Sensing danger, I sped away before he could finish."

She gave the delightful chuckle that always melted his heart and confessed,

"You see what a terrible woman I am. When we're married you'll never have a moment's peace. You should think carefully."

"As long as I have you for my wife, I shall care for nothing else," he breathed vehemently.

"And we shall be married very soon, so you'll see. Now, give me your arm, and let us go downstairs."

The dining room was magnificent, down the centre was an ornate table with equally ornate high-backed chairs.

One quick look showed Michael that no expense or trouble had been spared to produce a fine display.

Possibly Lord Challoner was showing him respect as a fellow Peer, but more likely he was making the point that this was the high life his lovely daughter was used to and her suitor should remember it.

He was certain of it a few minutes later when Lord Challoner entered the room and studied Michael's changed appearance.

He did not utter a word, but Michael had an uneasy feeling that he recognised the clothes as belonging to his dead son-in-law.

He took his seat at the head of the table and waved Michael to a seat at the opposite end.

Nothing could have been more courteous or correct than the way Michael was treated. On Lord Challoner's orders he was served first, as befitted the guest of honour.

His host always addressed him as 'Lord Belmont', making it plain to the servants that this was a man of title and distinction. The footmen seemed duly impressed and bowed after they had served him.

Again he had the uncomfortable feeling that Lord Challoner was silently telling him something.

At last dinner was finished as the last course was cleared away.

Lord Challoner gave a general smile and suggested,

"If you ladies would now care to depart and leave the gentlemen to their port?"

In a flurry of skirts they rose and left.

Lord Challoner then nodded to the butler to pour the port into two glasses.

It would have been simple for Michael to move to a seat nearer to his host, but no such suggestion was made.

He seemed content to shout the length of the table, which seemed to grow longer with every minute.

"So you fancy yourself in love with my daughter?"

"I love her dearly, sir."

"After just a few days?"

"I venture to hope that a few days is enough where my feelings are true. I dare to hope it is the same with her."

"She always was a headstrong girl. So you might deal well together."

A faint flicker of hope was now lit in Michael, then extinguished with the next words.

"But what sort of a life will she have with you, eh?"

"She will be a Countess."

"To be sure. I've been watching you this evening. You know all the right things to say and do. I've no doubt you are who you say you are. Well enough. But my girl has to live in a way that is proper to her station in life. What do you offer besides a title, hmm?"

"That I do not know, sir. But my father was well aware what was due to his name and whatever threats he made, I cannot believe he has carried them out."

"Then let us hope not. Otherwise you can forget all thought of marriage. Drink up and let's join the ladies."

He rose as he spoke, leaving Michael no choice but to do the same.

He was dismayed by the message he was receiving, and disgusted by his host's lack of manners.

But it might have been a lot worse, he reflected. He must go home quickly and discover how the land lies.

They joined the ladies and spent an uncomfortable half hour making conversation about nothing.

Then it was time for bed to everyone's relief.

As they were leaving Verna contrived to hang back and seize Michael's hand as he was leaving the room.

"What did my father say?" she asked, drawing him back inside.

"That there can be no marriage unless I can support you properly – "

Verna gave a cry, burying her face against him.

"But we don't have to heed him. I will decide who I marry, *not* Papa."

"My brave darling! But I don't want you to make sacrifices for me. Somehow I must find a way to win his approval."

"And if he will not give it? How can I lose you? How can I live without you? Oh, Michael, what are we to do?"

"I must return to my home tomorrow and see what has happened. Things may work out well.

"I love you, my darling Verna, and I know you love me. But if your father is against me – how can I possibly leave you? How can I go on living unless I can see you, speak to you and tell you – how much I love you?"

The words seemed to rush from his lips.

Verna could hear the pain not only in his words but in his eyes.

"I love you! I adore you!" she whispered. "If you have to find somewhere to work, whatever Papa may say to me, I will come and be with you.

"I have money of my own and if necessary I will work too. If we are together, nothing else really matters."

Michael stiffened.

"Do you really mean it, my darling?" he implored.

"I cannot lose you and you must not leave me. Oh, Michael, let's just run away and be married."

"How can you be so wonderful? How is it possible you love me so much that you would sacrifice everything to be with me?"

"That is all I want, all I care for," whispered Verna.

Michael's lips found hers.

He kissed her until they were both breathless.

At the same time, she felt as if she was giving him her heart and he was doing the same to her.

"I love you desperately, Michael" she sighed.

It was a little time later, when Michael had kissed her until it was impossible for them to be any closer.

"Good night my darling, Verna, let us live in hope. I am sure things will work out well for us."

He meant to be strong, but the sight of her and the feel of her in his arms was too much for him and suddenly he was kissing her again, passionately and ardently.

Kissing her until she felt she had completely melted into his body and they were not two people but one.

'I love you, Michael, I adore you!' Verna tried to say, but his lips held hers captive.

She could only think that she gave him not only her lips but her very heart.

"I will be waiting," she said at last, breathlessly. "I will come with you even if we have to hide in another part of the world. I love you! I belong to you and I want to be so much a part of you that no one could ever divide us or prevent us from being together."

"*Nothing*," he echoed. "Nothing."

On that vow they parted.

Later Michael lay in bed, looking into the darkness and dreaming of the happiness that might be his – if only things went well tomorrow.

*

Next morning he rose early and went downstairs to breakfast. As he had hoped nobody else was there except for Verna.

"I am going to drive you to your home, Michael."

"Won't your father object?"

"He won't know if we leave quickly."

Michael fetched his suitcase while Verna collected the car from the garage and they drove off together.

"There's a village just a few miles on, called Little Denning," Michael told her. "I will get out there and walk the last couple of miles."

"No, I can take you to your door."

"Better not. Besides I do think that you should go back quickly in case your father becomes angry."

She agreed reluctantly and a few minutes later they

rolled into Little Denning. They stopped and Michael went to the boot to collect his case.

"When will I see you again, Michael?" she begged.

"As soon as possible. I will come back as soon as I can. I adore and worship you, my darling Verna"

She blew him a kiss, then drove away, leaving him standing in the road, looking after her, smiling with joy.

After a few yards the road turned and as she swung the car round the corner, Verna managed to look sideways to find Michael and as she hoped he was still watching her.

She blew him another kiss and the next moment he was hidden from sight.

Michael found his walk to his home more pleasant than he had feared.

The sun was shining brightly, filling the world with light, making him feel contented. This was the countryside he had known as a child, where he had learned to ride and been part of a happy family.

Trouble had come eventually, but he could still look back on those childhood days as a happy time especially when his mother had been alive.

As he walked on he began to hear the distant tinkle of a brook and knew that this was where he had played as a lad. Now and then he passed people in the road and they hailed him cheerfully.

It was clear that they were glad to see him.

Despite his reputation as a reprobate he had always been popular with the tenants and workers on the estate.

His good nature and easy open-hearted generosity had seen to that.

His father had always been a man of upright virtue and his brother, Anthony, had a strong sense of duty. But neither of them had won the affection of the locals, as had Michael – the black sheep of the family.

As well as greetings they gave him interested looks, and he guessed they knew he had come to claim his title.

Of course they would not know how deeply he had quarrelled with his father or the threat to disinherit him.

As he walked on his conviction grew that all would indeed be well.

Papa would not have carried out his entire threat.

He was Lord Belmont, heir to all the Belmont lands and privileges. Papa might have left much of the money to Anthony, but he was too conscious of the significance of being an Earl to have left his elder son destitute.

He sat down by the brook, staring at the water.

'How did it happen?' he wondered. 'I know some of it was my fault, but not all. Papa always had a certain hostility to me all the time I was growing up.'

It was when he was older that he had realised his parents had never been particularly happy with each other.

His father was a most handsome man and women had always pursued him.

Looking back Michael could remember times when he had heard his mother scream at his father.

He had known if they were having a row, that some woman had received his father's attention in a way which his mother believed was an insult to her and a disgrace to the family.

His father began to stay away and when he returned he and his wife had seldom spoken to each other without quarrelling.

It was then that Michael had tried to help her and infuriated his father by doing so.

"It was your mother's idea to change the orders I had made about the crops," his father had said. "And you encouraged her. You are to do what *I* tell you to do."

"But you have been away, Papa. I could hardly ask you what I should do when I did not even know where you were staying."

"I gave my orders before I left," his father raged. "You and your mother have no right to change them."

"I only did what I thought was right, Papa."

"You did what *your mother* thought was right," his father answered furiously.

He had another reason for being hostile to Michael.

It soon became obvious that his son had inherited his own good looks. Ladies sighed after him and Michael realised that, incredibly, his father was jealous.

It was the dreary Anthony who was his favourite.

The quarrels increased until at last Michael spent as much time away from his home as possible. His own bad habits had developed out of boredom as much as anything.

He stayed on good terms with his mother, coming home to see her whenever he could, always making sure first that his father was absent.

He had been with her when she was dying, smiling at him with tender love.

"Try to forgive your father," she murmured.

"How can I ever forgive him?" he had demanded passionately. "He should be here with you now."

"Well maybe I can manage just as well without him as I have had to do many times. As long as you are here with me, my dear boy."

She sighed and continued,

"When your turn comes you will be a better Lord

Belmont than he ever was. I know that. I only pray that you will be lucky enough to find a wife that you love, who will be beside you for always."

"I will only marry a woman like you, Mama."

"As long as she loves you and you love her. That is all that matters. Be happy, my son. That is my last prayer for you."

Sitting on the bank now he spoke to the mother he still missed with all his heart.

'I will be so happy, Mama,' he vowed. 'Because I have found the perfect woman, just as you knew I would.'

CHAPTER SEVEN

He rose and walked firmly on.

Now he could see the great house in the distance, and stopped for a moment to take in the view of the honey-coloured building with its towers and turrets.

This lovely place was his and he was going to bring his bride here in pride and joy.

With his Verna at his side he would be a reformed character. Together they would rule the estate benignly, loved by all their dependants, as his mother had been.

His heart swelled with happiness and hope.

Another twenty minutes brought him to the house. Walking round it he came to the stables where he could see several grooms.

One looked up and a grin of delight spread across his face as he saw Michael.

"My Lord!" he bellowed. "*Welcome home!*"

They all came running towards him then, their faces full of joy.

"Thank goodness you're home, sir!" cried Bailey, the eldest groom. "Now things will be all right."

"I do hope so, Bailey."

"No one knew where you were, my Lord, and there be such dreadful rumours."

"Dreadful rumours have a habit of pursuing me," he remarked wryly. "I only learned of my father's death by accident. Has his funeral taken place yet?"

"No, my Lord. Mr. Snelkins, his man of business, insisted that nothin' could be done until you were found." Bailey lowered his voice. "That didn't please Mr. Anthony at all, sir. Proper put out he were."

"Really," Michael murmured.

"He's got a real temper and no mistake. But now you're here, it'll be all right."

"I'd better go inside and find out how things stand."

"Wait until this gets around the neighbourhood!" cried Bailey, doing a little dance that belied his age.

"Good times are coming now," exclaimed another and a little cheer went up from everyone.

It was obvious that none of them had heard rumours that he might be disinherited and Michael's spirits soared.

Servants always knew bad news before anyone and these grooms were making it clear that they accepted him as Lord Belmont – Master of all he surveyed.

He thought that the old house had never looked so beautiful as he returned hopefully to claim his birthright.

He headed for a side door that he knew was always open during the day and found it ajar.

The house was very quiet as he entered and slipped along the side passage until he came into the hall. Then he opened the door into the sitting room where most of his relations sat when they were not entertaining guests.

As he expected there were two of his sisters there who jumped up with a cry when they saw him.

"Oh, Michael, you have come at last!" exclaimed his eldest sister Jane. "We wondered where you were and when I tried to get in touch with you in London, they said you were abroad."

"I have only just returned from Paris. I saw in the newspaper what had happened to Papa."

"He died several days ago and we have been trying ever since to find you. You are the Earl now."

"I wonder just how much of an Earl I am," he said wryly.

"Why, whatever do you mean? Nothing can take your birthright from you."

Michael realised at once that Jane did not know of the trouble that might be awaiting him.

"I'll just take a quick look around," he muttered.

He went quietly up the stairs, wanting to reacquaint himself with his old home.

Here was his old room, looking bare and lonely, the bed stripped as though no occupant was ever expected to return. Was that what his father had been hoping?

But it was no longer his room. He was now Lord Belmont.

He headed along the corridor to the room that had belonged to his mother. Here he had sat with her as she lay dying and known, as he had always known, that he was her favourite child.

And then there was his father's room, the grandiose four-poster bearing the Belmont crest.

Michael stood before it, looking up at the crest.

'I may not have been too much good up to now,' he murmured. 'But I have changed. Love has done that to me, and with love's help I am going to be a credit to our lineage. And so is my wife – when she becomes my wife, which will be as soon as I can arrange it.'

"*Well, well, well!*"

He turned swiftly at the sound of the sneering voice from the doorway and sighed as he saw Anthony standing there, leaning against the wall.

"So the wanderer returns!"

"Yes, at last," Michael responded, refusing to be provoked. "It's good to be home."

"I wonder if you will always think so – "

He noticed that Anthony was already slightly tipsy, which meant that the more unpleasant side of his character was now to the fore. He was tall, lanky and unshaven, with a pallid, unhealthy appearance and sullen eyes.

"I thought you'd be gone for a lot longer," he said.

"You mean you hoped I would."

Anthony gave a quiet unpleasant laugh.

"Oh no, I have been looking forward to this. I have dreamed of the moment you returned home and I could tell you, face to face, exactly what our dear Papa has done."

An uneasiness began to stir inside Michael, but he tried to banish it.

"I know you were the favoured son, Anthony, and I daresay your inheritance is large."

"Large? It's total. The only thing you have left is the title. If Papa could have taken that from you, he would have done. As it is – it's all that you have. No money. No possessions. Nothing. You are *penniless*!"

Michael heard the words, but something inside him refused to believe them. The glorious dreams, so recently born, could not die in this terrible way.

Anthony could see his face growing paler and his glee increased.

"Welcome home, Lord Belmont. Welcome home, *Your Lordship.* That has a fine sound, doesn't it? Well, make the most of it, because it's all you have in the world."

"I don't believe you," Michael muttered stubbornly.

But he did.

"Believe what you like. You'll know everything soon enough when you hear the will. Snelkins, my man of business – "

"*Your* man of business?" Michael could not resist interrupting.

"Well, my dear fellow, I can hardly call him your man of business. You surely don't need one for a couple of hundred pounds a year."

"I have a little more than that," replied Michael.

"Oh yes, dear Mama left you *three* hundred a year, didn't she? What an immense fortune! I do believe that tradesmen contrive to live fairly well on it."

Tradesmen.

The word brought home to Michael how cruelly his fortunes had now changed. This was worse than anything he had imagined.

He had nothing to offer his beloved Verna.

Nothing.

"We weren't sure when you would get home – if you ever did," Anthony drawled on. "Papa's funeral has been delayed while we sought for you, but we could hardly have waited much longer. Luckily you are here, so all is well."

"All is well?" Michael echoed with soft fury. "You steal my inheritance and you say that *all is well*!"

"I stole nothing. Papa made his own decisions – "

"Influenced by you – "

"No, influenced by *you*, Michael. You are the one who quarrelled with him. He would not have disinherited you without good reason."

"I don't believe that he did disinherit me. I want to talk to the lawyer and hear every detail."

"Certainly. I sent for him as soon as I heard you arrive. Now you are here the full truth can come out."

"You mean the family does not know?"

"Not a thing. But they will know soon enough."

Anthony strolled away, leaving Michael no choice but to return to his old room. His head was spinning as he tried to tell himself that this could not be true.

And yet he knew it was.

Anthony would never have dared to say such things unless he was certain he could back them up.

'Oh, Verna, my Verna. What have I done?'

Dispiritedly he started to unpack his suitcase and was looking out of the casement window when he saw the lawyer arrive in his neat black carriage.

Glancing up, he saw Michael looking down at him, and hurriedly averted his gaze. That told Michael all he needed to know.

They all met in the library – Michael, tensed to hear the worst, the lawyer, very nervous, and Anthony, blatantly enjoying himself. The girls crowded around, wondering if their futures had been protected by their wayward father.

Mr. Snelkins addressed Michael in a hushed voice.

"I am so sorry that we have to meet under such sad circumstances, my – er – my Lord – "

"Stop wasting time," Anthony told him. "Just read the will. This has taken too long already."

"Er – yes, well – the will is very simple. The late Lord Belmont left his daughters twenty thousand pounds each. The rest of his estate goes to his son Anthony."

The girls gasped.

"No, that cannot be true," cried Jane. "Michael is the Earl, he cannot manage with nothing."

"But our Papa left him nothing," asserted Anthony. "Only the title, because he could not prevent that."

"The house – the land – "

"All mine," Anthony added softly. "Every brick, every blade of grass."

"But what will poor Michael do?" wailed Jane.

"Marry an heiress if he has any sense," Anthony snarled with a shrug.

Michael now rose and without another word left the room. His head was spinning and he was in a deep state of shock.

This could not be happening.

He had told himself that he was prepared for the worst, but he had never imagined this.

Cut off without a single penny, his only income the pittance from his mother. How could he marry his beloved Verna when he had so little?

He strode onto the drive and began to walk through the grounds, going faster and faster, never looking to see where he was, until he stopped and leaned against a tree.

The greenery around him was glorious. It should have been all his, but he had lost everything.

Now he would lose Verna too.

He was about to turn back despondently when he was alerted by the sound of horse's hooves.

Looking round he saw Verna galloping through the woods.

She looked so beautiful in her blue velvet riding habit that for a moment he could only stand and stare in admiration, forgetting all else.

She saw him and turned her horse, jumped to the ground and hurled herself into his arms.

Without a thought for anything but Verna, Michael kissed her fiercely and passionately.

"I couldn't bear waiting any longer," she told him. "Tell me what has happened and let's plan our future."

"My love, my love," he cried in a desperate voice, "we have no future. The news is worse than we could have dreamed. My father disinherited me completely. I have my title and nothing else."

"Oh no! How could he be so spiteful and horrible."

"Because that's the kind of man he was. I see now that he must have hated me. I have a hollow title and two hundred pounds a year."

"But people do live on two hundred pounds a year, and I have some money. We'll manage."

"You don't understand, my darling, I will have to find a job. If I marry I don't want to have to ask my wife for money, rather than her sharing what I possess."

"Oh, Michael, does money really matter when our hearts are so happy together? Nothing is more important than love!"

"You will never get your father to agree. He won't let you throw yourself away on a man who can give you nothing but himself."

"I don't want anything but you. If I was offered a million pounds to marry someone else, I would tell them all I wanted was you and your love for me."

She spoke very intensely.

"I adore you," he said fervently. "But I don't see how we can ever marry. There is too much in our way."

"Then we shall ignore it all. I love you with all my heart and soul. Once Papa realises how much you mean to me, he will accept you with open arms – for *my* sake."

She spoke with such conviction that he could only believe her. For a minute they stood, held in each other's arms in a tight embrace that seemed to promise forever.

But then Michael heard the sound of another horse approaching and looked up to find a sight that filled him with dread.

"I thought so," growled Lord Challoner, looking down at them. "When I heard that Verna had ridden off without the company of a groom, most improperly, I knew she would have come here."

"I had to come, Papa. Michael and I are engaged, and we mean to be married as soon as possible."

"I see."

His Lordship dismounted and faced Michael.

"Does this mean that all is well? Your father did not disinherit you?"

"No," admitted Michael. "He left me nothing at all. I have only my title and my willingness to work."

"Work?" Lord Challoner echoed, seeming puzzled by the word. "Just what kind work could you do without demeaning yourself and your title?"

"Oh, Papa!" Verna screamed impatiently. "What difference does all this make? Michael and I will face this together and I will help him in whatever he does."

"I see." Her father seemed to consider. "So if he earns his living as a shepherd, you will be a shepherdess? *How charming*!"

His voice was as cold as iron.

"I need hardly say," Michael declared stiffly, "that I would never ask Verna to do anything beneath her."

"Indeed. Then perhaps – "

Lord Challoner stopped, alerted by the sound of yet another horse approaching.

Looking up they could see Anthony, mounted on a magnificent grey that had once been Michael's favourite.

He was in slightly better condition, having sobered up and changed his clothes for something tidier.

He dismounted and faced them.

"Good day, Lord Challoner. It is too long since we last met."

"Yes, I am sorry I did not know your father better. We wasted too much time being hostile and spent too little time becoming acquainted at the end of his life. Now I would like to pay my respects at his funeral."

"You honour us. The funeral will be held soon."

Verna drew Michael aside.

"At least Papa is making an effort to be nice to your family," she whispered. "It's not like him."

Michael tried to look pleased for Verna's sake, but inwardly he was heartsick. Her father's sudden affability bore a more ominous interpretation.

His behaviour to Anthony, the one with wealth, was in sharp contrast to his frostiness towards Michael, the man with the empty title.

That was how he meant to be understood, Michael was sure. It was a message to himself.

And Anthony was none too subtly sending the same message. He was now the centre of attention, as was ably demonstrated by Lord Challoner's attitude to him.

He called Verna forth to talk to Anthony, which she did with courtesy but reserve.

Then, to Michael's horror, he heard Lord Challoner invite them for dinner that evening.

"Your whole family," he added.

Verna smiled at Michael, taking this as a hopeful sign and he tried to smile back.

But his heart was heavy, because instinct told him that this was an ominous development.

*

Dinner that night confirmed his worst fears.

It was ostensibly a quiet occasion out of respect for the family's grief over their dead father.

But it was obvious that Anthony meant to make the most of it, ordering his sisters to wear their best jewellery with their dark dresses.

He was elegant enough himself in his evening rig, sporting his late father's gold cufflinks.

Michael found out that he still possessed a tolerable evening dress, but his cufflinks were modest for an Earl.

"It's all right," he told Jane, when she was upset for his sake. "It's the way things are now."

"But *you* are the Earl," his sister protested tearfully.

"Yes, I am the Earl. But that's all I am. Oh, Jane, I've just started to realise how little a title means. If it isn't backed up with wealth, it is only hollow words. And the worst of it is, it's all my own fault."

"Papa was never fair to you, Michael," she added loyally. "He always made a favourite of Anthony."

"Perhaps, but if I am honest, I gave him plenty of excuse to turn against me. I lived a dissolute life, thinking only of enjoying myself. Now I am paying the price. I just wish that others did not have to pay too."

Pulling himself together, he suggested,

"It's time we were going. It will be a very difficult evening, but I must put a brave face on it."

They travelled in the big carriage with the family crest on the side. As they approached Challoner Abbey, Michael could see that it was ablaze with light.

The elaborate front door was open and six footmen in powdered wigs already stood on the front steps.

Clearly Lord Challoner had decided to do things in style.

A devil seemed to have got into Anthony. As they climbed out of the coach, he deferred ostentatiously to his brother.

"After you, *my Lord*," he proclaimed.

"Stop that – " muttered Michael.

"But *nothing* is too good for the new Earl."

So that's his game, Michael thought with a sinking heart. His spiteful brother would lose no opportunity to underline their different fortunes.

Then everything went out of his head as he saw his beloved appear on the steps and hurry down to him, her arms outstretched, her face full of joy.

She greeted his two sisters pleasantly and smiled at Anthony though with some reserve. As they ascended the steps together he realised that she was regarding the whole matter as settled and this dinner merely as a formality.

He only hoped that she was right, but his heart was full of dread.

On the surface all was well.

Lord Challoner had exerted himself to honour his guests, which was as it should be. But Michael sensed an undercurrent. There was an ostentatious display of wealth, a parade of extravagant style that he still felt was meant as a signal to himself.

Like the Belmont ladies, the Challoner ladies wore their very best jewellery. Verna was dazzling in diamonds, while her sisters wore pearls, rubies and sapphires.

Michael guessed that this too had been an order.

Lord Challoner was letting him know that this kind of life was what he expected for his daughter, and the man who could not provide it need not aspire to be her husband – no words were necessary.

Lord Challoner treated Michael as the chief guest, addressing him as 'Lord Belmont', with only the faintest emphasis on 'Lord'. But his eyes glinted.

From time to time Michael glanced across the table to where his Verna sat, poised and beautiful, occasionally smiling at him.

And his heart ached.

When the ladies had left the gentlemen to their port Lord Challoner began to talk about running a great estate, almost as though he had not heard that Michael had been disinherited.

Michael listened to him stony-faced and dreadfully aware of Anthony, watching him across the table with a spiteful smile on his face.

At last it was time to join the ladies.

As soon as he entered the drawing room, Michael went to Verna, who looked up at him quickly.

"Is Papa behaving well to you?" she enquired.

"He is being perfectly civil."

She took his hand to draw him to the door.

"Come with me," she whispered. "I simply must be alone with you."

Quickly they left the drawing room and slipped into the dimly lit library.

Then she was in his arms, kissing him as fervently as he was kissing her.

"Everything's going to be all right," she murmured. "As long as we still love each other, nothing can go wrong. Let's get married very soon."

"My darling Verna, you are so brave. If only I had your courage."

"It comes from you. Oh, kiss me, kiss me!"

He did so, pulling her hard against him and putting his whole heart and soul into the kiss.

For a few blinding moments they were transported through the stars to Heaven.

But then, as he had always known would happen, Heaven was snatched away by an ominous sound.

The click of the library door closing.

Looking up, Michael saw with a sinking heart that Lord Challoner had come into the room and was standing there watching them with cold hard eyes.

"You must forgive me for intruding," he remarked tartly, "but I do have the strongest objection to having my daughter seduced under my roof."

"Papa!" Verna burst out indignantly.

"Be silent!" her father snapped at her. "You should be ashamed to behave like this, throwing yourself at him."

"I will not be silent," she cried out. "And I am not throwing myself at Michael, because he loves me and we are to be married."

Lord Challoner now looked Michael up and down contemptuously.

"Yes, so you told me earlier, but do you seriously intend to go through with such a marriage that will lead my daughter into poverty and misery."

"Papa, you are *so* unfair!"

"Am I? Then perhaps I have been misinformed. Maybe a new inheritance has come to light, meaning that you can afford to support my daughter?"

"No sir. It is just as I told you earlier."

"Then I am afraid that marriage is completely out of the question. Did you really think I would allow one of my family to wed into squalor?"

"But Papa, we do love each other," Verna screamed frantically. "Why can't you believe me?"

"I do believe you," her father replied loftily. "But I cannot see what relevance it has? Marriage is about far more than love, as you will soon learn when I have found a suitable husband for you."

"No! I will never marry anyone else. Michael tell him that he cannot stop us."

Michael was silent.

"*Michael*!" she howled in despair.

"My love," he choked, "What your father says is true. I cannot marry you into poverty. I have nothing to offer you."

"Nothing but your love! Nothing but yourself."

"I am afraid that 'myself' does not amount to very much," he responded wryly.

"And your love?" she challenged him. "Does that not amount to very much?"

"You'll never know how much I love you," he said, barely able to speak. "You are my life – *my everything*. I love you too deeply to do you the injury of marrying you."

"Thank you, sir," rasped Lord Challoner. "I'm glad to see that you have at least that much honour."

"Papa!" Verna burst out in anguish.

"No gentleman of honour could marry you under these circumstances. The matter is now concluded."

"It is *not* concluded," Verna yelled hotly.

"Yes," stated Michael, very pale. "It is. We cannot marry."

"But I don't care about money. I have some of my own – "

"Supplemented by a generous allowance from me,"

her father came in brutally. "An allowance that will stop if you do anything at all foolish. You will not like living in poverty, my girl."

"You need have no fear," asserted Michael. "My mind is made up. There will be *no* marriage."

Verna gave a cry and buried her face in her hands.

Michael made an instinctive move to her then drew back, knowing that he no longer had the right to take her in his arms to caress and comfort her.

She was lost to him forever.

CHAPTER EIGHT

At the end of the week the late Lord Belmont was buried in the local Church, which was almost too small to accommodate such a large crowd. Nobody wanted to miss such a notable occasion as the funeral of a great aristocrat and extravagant personality.

Nor were they going to lose the chance to witness the hint of tasty scandal that had made itself known across the district.

It was said that the two brothers had tried to murder each other in a duel and that tragedy had only been averted by Lord Challoner hurling himself between them.

Nobody really believed the story, least of all those who knew Anthony and recalled what a cry-baby he had been all his life. A whiner and a sneak, so different from the handsome and upstanding Michael.

Rumours circulated that Lady Verna had confined herself to her room, sobbing and in this rumour there was some truth.

The chief families of the district were all present, including the Challoners, swathed in black as though their nearest and dearest lay in the coffin.

When the Belmont family arrived all eyes turned to look at Michael, the very picture of the new Earl. He was dressed in black and dreadfully pale, looking neither to the right nor the left.

Michael saw Lord Challoner as soon as he entered the Church and he instinctively looked for Verna.

At first he just could not tell her from the others, all in black and covered in veils, but then he saw that one of them was turning in his direction in agonised intensity.

And he knew that it was Verna and the knowledge smote him to the heart.

He faced the fact that all was over between them and during the last two days he had told himself that he would be forced to learn to live with his pain.

But when he saw her there, yearning towards him, he knew that the pain would never end in all his life.

The Funeral Service began and the Parson intoned words from the Bible. To Michael's fevered imagination certain phrases stood out starkly –

"*We have brought nothing into the world and it is certain we can carry nothing out. The Lord gave, and the Lord hath taken away.*"

He had nothing because everything had been taken away from him. In fact he had less than nothing because he had discovered the love of his life – only to lose her.

Somewhere he felt he could hear his father cackling malevolently at the terrible deed he had done.

'Goodbye, Father,' he thought. 'I only wish I could grieve for you, but I cannot – not after what you have done to me and the pleasure I am sure that you took in it!'

Through the heavy black veil her father had insisted on her wearing, Verna tried to see Michael, tried to get him to meet her eyes, but it was impossible.

She could barely make him out, although she knew he would be sitting in the place of honour – the new Lord Belmont, entering upon his grandeur. Except that it was really a cruel joke.

At last the coffin was carried out of the Church and past the cemetery into the elaborate mausoleum where the Belmonts were always interred.

"*Dust to dust, ashes to ashes,*" recited the Parson.

'*Ashes,*' Michael thought.

It was a perfect description of the life that faced him now. He had not just lost his rightful position, but he must be separated from the love of his life, for he knew he could never take his darling Verna into poverty.

He ventured to turn his eyes towards her, willing her to look at him and at last she turned her head.

But he could only see her veil. He wondered how well she could see him. Did she know of his anguish?

But of course she did. If her eyes could not tell him, her heart would.

If the funeral was painful, the reception afterwards was a thousand times worse.

It was held in the Great Hall, under the portraits of the notable Belmonts of history. Some had been ministers of Kings and Queens, one had been a great explorer.

They looked down loftily on the man with the title but no money and his brother with the money and no title.

Anthony was indeed behaving beautifully, holding back, deferring to Michael, whom he continually referred to as *Lord* Belmont. Michael was not fooled. He knew what Anthony was doing.

By now the whole neighbourhood knew the truth about their respective positions.

He even had the effrontery to approach Michael and put a hand on his shoulder.

"Courage, my dear brother," he said. "This is a sad time for all the family, but we must all endure everything together."

"*Together* is hardly the right word – "

"But surely you don't think I am going to leave you

destitute? You are still my brother. I have a plan that will make things better for you."

Michael was scarcely able to believe what he was hearing.

Was he really preparing to share his inheritance?

If so, he and Verna might still find some way to be together.

Wild hope stirred within him.

"Do you really mean it?" he asked.

"Of course I do, Michael. Did you think I would let you starve? This place is going to need an estate manager and who better than you?"

Michael stared at Anthony as the enormity of his proposal hit him.

"*Your* estate manager?" he blurted out at last. "You want me to work for you as a servant?"

"I'll pay you good wages and you can live in the two rooms over the stable – "

He broke off and backed away, suddenly alarmed by the look in Michael's eyes.

"Be careful," Michael told him softly, "or I may be tempted to wring your neck here and now. It would be no more than you would deserve. Work for you? Live over the stables on the estate that should be mine? Were you mad when you thought of that idea?"

"I only want to help you," stammered Anthony.

"You only want to humiliate me and I shall never forget it. I would sooner starve in a ditch than accept your offer. Now, get out of my sight!"

Anthony scuttled away.

Suddenly he could no longer bear his surroundings, the many eyes regarding him furtively.

He now walked straight out of the room, knowing that he left behind a buzz of speculation, but past caring.

He found the library empty and sank into the big leather sofa, staring out into the distance, a prey to the most unbearable bitterness.

This was the end of all his dreaming.

His last chance had been the hope of finding some generosity in his brother. But it had been a foolish hope, and there was nothing left for him but to face reality.

He had already partly faced it by packing a bag and leaving it here – in the library – where he could take it and slip away quickly.

Even at the last his heart had treasured a dream that it would not be necessary, that something would happen to save him and his darling Verna from the wretched fate that awaited him.

Now he knew that would not happen and realised that he must leave fast.

But first he must say a terrible goodbye.

He heard the click of the door and the next moment Verna was beside him on the sofa and in his arms.

"Darling, tell me what has happened," she begged. "What were you talking about with your brother?"

"He was offering me a job – estate manager, living in two rooms over the stables."

"We could manage – "

"Do you think I would ever take you to live in such a way?" he demanded, almost violently. "Is that the kind of man you think I am?"

"I'll tell you the kind of man I think you are," she answered softly, "you are the man I love and the only man I will ever love. I think you are strong and brave but so am I, and I know that if I cannot become your wife, then my life is *over*."

He loved her even more for these loyal words.

Her willingness to face any hardship rather than be parted from him made him want to fall at her feet. But he refused to yield to his feelings. What he had to do was terrible, but it must be done and the sooner he made an end the better for them both.

Taking a deep breath, he forced himself to say,

"Nonsense!"

She looked up at him, startled.

"Of course your life isn't over," he said in a voice that he tried to make harsh. "You will forget me in no time and find a man who *is* suitable."

"*Michael!*"

Her cry of such pain pierced his heart, but he forced himself not to weaken.

"We cannot afford to be sentimental about this," he continued. "We enjoyed a pleasant flirtation, but it's over now and now we go our separate ways."

"I don't believe you," she whispered. "You are just saying this for my sake. You are trying to put me off – "

"I am trying to save you from pain and regret," he growled.

"There would be neither if you love me as I love you," she affirmed strongly.

He closed his eyes, recognising that the greatest sacrifice of his life was being demanded of him.

At all costs he must save his Verna from the life of misery that would await her if they married – poor, derided by the world, perhaps sick if he could not afford to buy her good medical care.

"Well, then," he replied, speaking as lightly as he could manage, "*perhaps I do not.*"

"*What* – what did you say?" Verna howled, unable to believe that she had heard him properly.

"I am saying that it's time to be realistic, my dear. We've been fond of each other, but let's not fool ourselves that we have found a great death-defying love. Such things exist only in novels. A marriage between us would have been very nice, if it had been possible. But it isn't and we must each find another life."

"*No,*" she cried, backing away from him wild-eyed. "I just don't believe this. You are being generous, trying to protect me."

Out of sight he clenched his hands into fists.

How well she knew him, far too well to be so easily deceived! But it meant that he must try all the harder to convince her.

Inwardly he prayed for the strength to be cruel.

"Heaven save me from a woman who cannot face facts," he said, infusing his voice with a touch of languid boredom. "Look, my dear, it's over. It's time for each of us to find a new life and I do not intend mine to be in a hovel struggling to make ends meet.

"There's a world to be discovered by a man with brains and enterprise. I might even become a professional gambler. If I concentrate really hard, I could probably live well. Or perhaps I'll go to America and make my fortune there. But whichever I choose, I need to be free from – shall we say – entanglements?"

"Is that all I am? *An entanglement*?"

"Well, let's just say that I've been giving the matter some thought and it might be that this new life with suit me better than many domestic ties. I have always enjoyed my freedom and I always will. It's true that your company made me dream of other things – briefly. But I am the man I am, and I am not going to change now."

"No," she whispered. "No, don't say these things. They're not true – they can't be – "

"You have had a lucky escape, if only you would realise it. You are meant for a respectable life with a solid husband and a nursery. For me, it's the open road."

"You mean that?" Verna whispered, looking at him from eyes full of cruel disillusion. "You *really* mean that?"

Now was his last chance to tell her the truth – that he did not mean a word of it, that he would worship her until his last moment, although after today he might never see her again.

It took all the strength he could muster not to fall at her feet begging for her love and forgiveness, imploring her to run away with him and stay with him forever.

"Yes," he muttered coolly. "I really mean it."

He wanted to cry out – '*don't believe me.*'

But all this was for nothing, unless he could *make* her believe him.

If only she would say something instead of looking at him as if her heart had completely turned to stone. Or even do something, accuse him, insult him – *anything*.

"I think it's time I was going now," he said. "I will not be staying for the rest of this charade. I have got my things – "

He indicated the packed bag by his feet.

"You're just going to walk out without a goodbye?"

"I've left farewell letters to my sisters. The others will be glad if I don't reappear. Certainly Anthony will. *And* your father."

"And if I hadn't happened to walk in when I did, would you have bothered with me?" she asked in a voice that was beginning to harden.

"Probably not. We had a good time together, but all things come to an end. We can say our goodbyes now."

"And I'll say it gladly," she fumed as her fury rose. "I see the truth about you now. You're nothing but a cheap trickster with no honour or morals! You made me love you to pass the time, didn't you?"

He recovered enough to blurt out,

"You must admit – it passed the time beautifully."

The words were scarcely out of his mouth before he was reeling back under a slap across the face that was more powerful than he would have expected from any woman.

But this woman was under the influence of violent emotions.

"I thought you were different from other men," she raged. "I loved you – at least, I loved what I thought you were. But your heart is hollow and empty!"

"All the better for you – to have escaped from me," he stuttered, resisting the temptation to rub his cheek.

"I would have given up everything for you," she seethed, eyes flashing, "and never counted the cost. If you loved me, any sacrifice would have been worth it.

"But I see now what a fool I was to give my heart to a man who didn't know how to value it. I'll never make such a dreadful mistake again, not for you or any man. If this is what love is like, I want *none* of it."

"Don't say that," he begged. "There will still be love in your life – "

"Be silent!" she commanded. "How dare you say that to me! How dare you presume to tell me what my life will be! You can have no idea what you have done, how I despise you and all men."

"Excellent," he just managed to say. "If you have learned to despise me, that's probably best for both of us."

Scarcely knowing what he did, he picked up his bag and walked out of the room, then out of the house, careful to avoid anyone.

He slipped out by a side door and began to run. He ran and ran, faster and faster, desperate to get away from this place that he could no longer bear, feeling as though he was running for his life.

At last when he was deep in the forest, he stopped and leaned against a tree.

He felt drained and exhausted, bereft of everything that made life worth living.

The scene with Verna had been agonising.

He had known that it had to be done for the sake of his darling, but it had torn him apart to treat her so. The memory of her face, regarding him with misery and hate, tortured him.

It was the last sight of her he would ever see.

He was glad of the stinging in his face where she had slapped him. It was the last touch he would ever have from her.

Now he began to understand how his life had really changed.

He had not taken a horse from the stables with him as he would once have done.

It began to pour with rain.

He pulled his collar up around his ears and walked on, trying to ignore the storm that pounded him, growing heavier with every moment.

Absorbed by so many dismal thoughts, he realised that he had almost reached the little town of Halton and had no idea where he would go then.

It must be somewhere where he was not known.

'I must now go abroad,' he decided. 'That is the only way to begin a new life.'

And the thought came to him – perhaps he should leave England altogether and sail for America.

His mother's small legacy had enabled him to take some money with him, enough to survive for a while and probably enough for a passage to America.

He trudged on till he reached the station, where he bought a ticket to London.

Once there he caught an omnibus to Euston Station where he bought a second class ticket to Liverpool. From that Northern port the ships departed for America.

On arrival he headed straight for the port, anxious to make his decision final before he could weaken.

He checked the departure times and discovered that the *SS Caledonia* was due to leave the following day.

He had enough money to pay for Steerage. He had heard that this was fairly primitive, but there was nothing for it. This was a new life and one in which the comforts he had been used to were gone – as was the love.

But he would not weaken. If the life that stretched ahead of him was tough, then he would be tougher.

He would become a man Verna could be proud of, although she would never know.

Reaching into his pocket he drew out some money and joined the queue at the ticket window.

Soon his fate would be sealed for ever.

He would be on his way to America and nobody in this country would ever hear from him again.

'Verna darling, my own true love,' he murmured, 'goodbye. Goodbye for ever in this world. Please God we shall meet again in another life.'

From the small casement window Verna watched as Michael walked away. With all her heart she longed to run after him, tell him again of her love and make him return.

But she knew it was useless.

He had made his decision and instinct told her that beneath his charm and good looks lay a man of steel.

She would be as strong as he, she vowed.

But when he was out of sight, her resolution broke and she flew out into the garden.

"*Michael*!" she cried in agony. "Come back, come back to me!"

But there was so sign of him and now the storm had started, thundering down and soaking her to the skin.

"Michael!" she bawled. "*Come back, Michael.*"

But he had gone forever.

She ran on and on until her strength was gone and she collapsed against a tree, weeping.

"Michael, Michael, do come back to me, my love. Don't do this to us. How will I live without you?"

Slowly she slid down the trunk, until she subsided into a heap at the bottom and stayed there unable to move, sobbing her heart out.

Now she was sure that her life was over.

"Hallo! *Hallo!*"

She tensed at the sound of a man's voice, fearful it was her father. But through the falling rain she could make out the sight of Anthony approaching her.

"Lady Verna," he called out sharply, as he dropped down on one knee beside her. "What are you doing here? You will catch your death of cold."

"I don't care," she replied huskily. "*He* has gone."

"Gone? Who?"

"Michael. He says he is leaving for good, because there can be no future for us now. I may never know what becomes of him and I care for nothing now."

Anthony was silent.

If she had been watching him, Verna would have seen a cool calculation in his eyes, but she had buried her face into her hands, and when Anthony spoke she was only aware of something in his voice that sounded like kindness.

"You must not say that, Lady Verna. If you don't care for your own fate, you should remember that there are those who care a great deal for you, who would be greatly pained if anything bad were to happen to you."

"The worst tragedy in the whole world has already happened. What more can there be?"

"You could get pneumonia from being out here in the cold. That must be prevented at all costs. Let me help you to your feet."

He raised her and held her steady lest she fall.

"Oh, Heavens, look at me!" she exclaimed. "What will my father say when he sees me?"

"He must not see you," Anthony declared. "Let us return now to the house and I will send you home in my car. When you have gone I'll tell your father that you were feeling ill and had to leave. By the time he's followed you home you will have been able to change out of your wet clothes and he need know nothing about this."

"Oh, yes, yes, please let's do that," she gasped.

"Take my arm."

She did so, and they walked slowly away together. She knew that this was Anthony, whom Michael regarded as an enemy, but for the moment she could only feel his kindness.

He attended to her solicitously on the journey back, speaking gently. Once he addressed her as plain 'Verna' and immediately corrected himself to 'Lady Verna.'

"Please call me Verna," she said. "You are being so good to me."

"I cannot bear seeing you in such distress. Look, we are nearly there. Stay here amongst the trees so that nobody sees you, while I arrange for the car."

In a few moments the car was there.

Anthony spoke to the chauffeur, handed her in the back and climbed in beside her.

"I will come as far as your front door, Verna, then leave you to be cared for by your servants."

She nodded.

Despair was starting to overtake her and she could not speak. She longed to disappear right out of sight of the world, where she could weep her heart out.

But she smiled politely at Anthony.

She closed her eyes tightly and had no idea how long it took to reach her home.

But then suddenly they arrived and Winifred was running out, looking anxious.

Anthony handed her out of the car and bade her a polite farewell.

"Trust me to say everything that is necessary," he said. "Very soon I shall do myself the honour of calling to enquire after you."

He saw her safely into Winifred's hands.

Then he got back into the car and was driven away.

CHAPTER NINE

Michael thought he must be dreaming.

A small girl was looking down at him and when he opened his eyes, she rose, crying,

"Papa, Mama, he is awake."

She stood back as a middle-aged man and woman came bustling into the room. Like their daughter they had faces beaming with goodwill.

"Why, that's so much better," exclaimed the man. "We thought you would never open your eyes."

"Who – who are you?" whispered Michael. "And where am I?"

"I am Henry Sanson," the man declared. "Here is my wife, Irene and my little daughter Penny and this is our house in Liverpool."

"I am still in Liverpool?" he choked. "But – I was going to America – on the *SS Caledonia*. I do remember standing in the queue to buy a ticket, but then – "

"You were attacked. Someone hit you on the head and ran off with your money."

"The ship – "

"It sailed this morning."

Michael groaned.

"Well, I have no money anyway. But what am I doing here?"

"I had you brought to my home."

"That is very kind of you, sir." He closed his eyes. "You did tell me your name – I apologise – "

"Never mind now," the older man said soothingly. "The doctor says you need rest, then you will be all right."

It was bliss to sink back into sleep.

His head was aching, his heart was broken and he longed for oblivion.

When he woke again it was dark.

Henry was sitting by the window, looking out at the night, but he rose and came towards the bed.

"That's better. We'll soon have you on your feet. The first thing is to get some food into you."

Over the next few days they tended him as lovingly as if they had been his own family. Henry's kind heart had made him become Michael's protector.

He was a businessman who had started in a poor way, selling cheap goods from a barrow in the market and risen as far as his limited education would allow. Marriage to a woman with a sharp brain had helped and they now owned two shops overlooking the port.

"I'd just been round collecting the takings," he told Michael, "and I stopped to look at the ships, as I often do. I long to see America, but at my age I can only dream.

"As I was turning away I saw a commotion through the door of the ticket office and two men running off down the street. I looked in and there you were on the floor with blood streaming from your head."

"I dread to think what would have happened to me but for your kindness," said Michael. "But, as you know, I have no money to repay you."

"Have I asked for money from you?" Henry puffed, preparing to be offended. "What does money have to do with it?"

"Forgive me," Michael apologised hastily. "I did you an injustice."

"There is a small favour you could do me," Henry added thoughtfully. "But we'll talk about it later."

He waited another two days before taking Michael to see the new shop he had bought and was hoping to open soon selling 'fashionable' goods.

"You are obviously a gentleman," remarked Henry. "You would bring in a good class of clientele. I don't just mean behind the counter. You would be the manager and run the place."

"But you know nothing at all about me," protested Michael. "I might be on the run from the law."

"Well if you are, the law has had plenty of chance to catch up with you. They don't seem to be in too much of a hurry!"

"If you're going to trust me handling your money," Michael replied thoughtfully, "then you really must know everything about me. Only promise never to repeat it – "

"Word of honour."

"Then I will tell you."

He told Henry his story, omitting no detail that was to his discredit, describing the disgraceful circumstances that had caused his father to disinherit him.

He concealed his true identity, nor did he speak of Verna, but he said openly that he had been forced to accept employment as a chauffeur.

"I have spent years living in and out of gambling dens and living on my wits," he admitted. "It has been a shameful life."

But Henry had his own way of looking at things and he merely observed thoughtfully,

"You must be very good with figures."

"No man can calculate odds as precisely as I can," Michael told him with a wry smile.

"Excellent. Then nobody will be able to fool you, which is exactly what I need. We'll start work as soon as you are fully recovered. That is – if you agree."

Michael drew a long breath as he looked at the new crossroads suddenly revealed before him, but he realised that there was no real choice.

Fate had snatched away his prospects in America, but it had also offered him a new life among good people.

And Liverpool was sufficiently far from his home to protect his identity.

"Very well, I'll do it," he cried. "If you are so sure you can trust me not to make you bankrupt."

Henry beamed.

"We're going to be the success of the age!"

From that moment they never looked back.

Michael threw himself into the business with gusto, discovering that he had a talent for it. While the new shop was being set up, he spent some time in Henry's other two shops, learning how things were done.

He soon discovered that Henry's bookkeeping was a shambles, partly because he was being cheated by one of his staff.

Sensing retribution the employee escaped, leaving Michael to scramble back through a myriad transactions to put the Company's affairs straight.

At last he managed it all and put everything onto a steady footing.

Profits improved.

Henry wore a permanent smile.

Michael remained in the family home, paying Mrs.

Sanson for his lodging and adding to his value by teaching mathematics to the three Sanson children.

This endeared him to their mother, who was keen on female education and was contemptuous of the 'footling nonsense' too often considered good enough for girls.

It was a great day when the third shop was opened. While the other two sold basic goods, this one appealed to those who were enjoying increasing wealth.

From the first moment it was a success.

Michael had found his new life and it was, in many ways, a contented one. He was busy, he knew himself to be useful and he had friends who cared for him. He told himself that he was a lucky man.

It was only sometimes, when he was alone, that he sat in the fading light and thought of another life – and the happiness that had almost been his.

Occasionally he would allow himself to think about Verna and envisage her lovely face smiling at him, sweet and full of love.

He would wonder where she was and what she was doing. Did she still remember him or did she love another?

Then he would draw a long shuddering breath and banish her image, unable to bear the pain of missing her.

At last he would open his eyes and look around at the new life that now seemed so satisfactory. He could see how little it really meant beside all he had lost.

And his heart would break.

*

Before she left the house Verna took a last look at herself in the mirror to ensure that she was neat and tidy.

Everything was in place.

Her riding habit was cut to perfection, her hat was perched atop her hair, scarf perfectly tied beneath her chin.

126

"You look beautiful," he father told her warmly.

"Thank you, Papa," she acknowledged dutifully.

In fact she was checking her appearance merely for propriety, not looks. It was only with Michael that she had cared about looking beautiful. But she did not say this to Papa, because it would have made him angry.

Six months had passed by since her life had ended with Michael's departure.

Six long months when she had walked and talked, smiled and danced, presented a perfect face to the world.

Six months when there was nothing but emptiness inside her.

Would it never end? she wondered. Would her life always be a lonely desert because the one man she could ever love had flown away?

Some parts of that fateful day lived vividly in her mind, whilst some were bathed in mist.

She vaguely remembered the journey home in the car, soothed by Anthony's kindliness. She was shivering violently and he sat in the car holding her in his arms as a brother might have done.

What would she have done without him, she was wondering now. He had kept her safe until they reached her home and he had handed her to Winifred, saying that she had been overcome with faintness and promising that he would smooth everything over.

And he had done so.

When the rest of her family returned she had lain in bed and heard Winifred talking to her father, refusing to let him in to disturb her.

"All she needs is rest, my Lord, and I'm going to see that she gets it," she had firmly laid down the law.

Even Lord Challoner did not contend with Winifred when she was in a formidable mood.

"Then I will leave her with you," he replied.

Mercifully he had gone away, leaving Verna to sob her heart out.

Michael had gone forever and she would never see him again.

After the first shock she had been able to discount his cruel insistence that he did not love her.

Her heart knew him well enough to believe that he had spoken in this way from generous motives. It was his way of releasing her to go on with life and love again.

But for her to love again was quite impossible and he should have known that.

Next day Anthony had come calling. His manner was polite and reserved, courteous and considerate.

He desired only to enquire after her health and she had no hesitation in going riding with him. It was a relief to be away from the house.

At first she was cautious, remembering Michael's rage against his brother, how he distrusted him and blamed him for daring to offer him the post of estate manager.

But Anthony was persistent in his self-reproach.

"I was searching for a suitable way of helping him. That was my only fault. But I was unforgivably clumsy. I should have thought how it would look to him. And you – what must you think of me?"

"You meant only to help," she said softly. "None of us can imagine how things look to him now."

There was comfort in his company. She could talk to him about Michael and he would listen for as long as she wanted.

They spent many hours riding together, sometimes galloping, sometimes cantering gently, then stopping to sit quietly beside a stream and talk.

Verna constantly wanted to find out if Michael had sent a letter to his home, but there was always nothing.

"He doesn't write to us," Anthony told her with an air of sadness. "Not even to his dear sisters who he was so fond of. I keep hoping you can give us news of him."

"I have had no letters," she sighed. "Nothing. Not a word. He said our parting was for ever and he meant it. Unless Papa – "

She fell silent, unwilling to voice her fears that her father would intercept her letters, but she felt that Anthony would understand.

"We must both of us wait and hope," he suggested.

They rode home to find Lord Challoner watching from a window. He greeted Anthony in a friendly spirit and invited him to stay for lunch. He accepted and spent the meal laughing and joking with the whole family.

Watching him, Verna felt safe. He seemed such a good friend.

She knew nothing of the brief meeting between her father and Anthony, just before he left the house.

"I don't have to tell you how very pleased I am to see the friendship between you and Verna," Lord Challoner observed quietly. "I hope it proceeds well."

"It does, but I am forced to be patient," Anthony murmured. "I beg you to say nothing to her prematurely."

"Surely she must be over your brother by now," he exclaimed.

"I'll bide my time. To alert her to my thoughts too soon could frighten her away."

"Then she is very foolish. You are the catch of the neighbourhood."

"Not in every respect. I have the family fortune, but Michael has the title."

"But you are the better man and that's what I want for my daughter."

Lord Challoner attempted a feeble joke,

"Perhaps Verna should be careful lest you switch your attention to one of her sisters!"

"Oh no," Anthony said at once. "I shall not do that. My decision is made, but I am content to wait for hers."

But Verna knew nothing of this plan.

She knew only that Anthony was gentle, kindly and always at her service.

When a near neighbour gave a huge ball in his great country house, she was reluctant to attend.

"If you stay away when the rest of your family goes, you will draw attention to yourself," Anthony pointed out. "Surely you do not wish to be the object of gossip?"

"Oh no! How horrible!" Verna shuddered. "But to be stared at by all those people – "

"Will you trust me to take care of you?" Anthony asked. "You know I am your friend."

At the ball they danced together and people said what a lovely couple they made.

Verna looked magnificent in a gown of blue satin, a diamond tiara on her head.

After that they danced together often and gradually she became aware that people were smiling at them in a significant manner.

They were perceived as a couple.

Now she blamed herself for not having thought of this possibility, but it was so plain to her that there could be no other man but Michael that she had assumed it was as plain to everyone else.

She wondered if Anthony had fallen into this error. Could he really be only the kindly brother he seemed?

She was thinking of this today as she checked her appearance in the hall mirror under the eyes of her father.

"You outshine all other women," he told her. "I'm sure that Anthony thinks so."

"Papa, please! It isn't like that between Anthony and me. He is my good friend. He understands how I feel about – "

"Come, come! That business was over long ago."

"Not in here," she insisted, laying her hand over her breast. "How can you know me so little?"

"But you cannot pine for one man for ever!" Lord Challoner asserted. "You have your life ahead of you."

"Or behind me," she added softly.

She went to meet Anthony with the determination to clear up any misunderstanding, but there was no need for her to speak.

He had tired of waiting and made her his proposal as soon as they were alone.

"No, please – " she choked. "I never meant to mislead you – you know my feelings – "

"I know about your love for my brother, but I had dared to hope that time might make you look on me with a more favourable eye. I do not ask you to love me as you loved him. I am content to be your devoted slave."

"You deserve better, Anthony. You must have a woman who truly loves you for yourself."

"But perhaps I could teach you to love me, Verna. Together we could embark on a long journey of discovery, taking us to the farthest reaches of love – "

Before she knew what he meant to do he had seized her in his arms and was kissing her passionately.

With all her strength Verna struggled free and gave him a resounding slap across the face.

"Never do that – again," she screamed breathlessly.

"Oh, how mistaken in you I was! I love Michael and only Michael. There will never be another love for me. I would die for him. Now do you *understand*?"

His face turned pale, but he had control of himself. Anthony was not the man to lose sight of his object for the sake of a moment's temper.

"Forgive me, Verna," he asked her quietly. "I will escort you home."

On the journey he did not displease her by reverting to the subject. He spoke of indifferent matters until they arrived and then he bade her good day and rode away.

At Belmont Park he was greeted by the news that his valet, Ratby, had returned after a week's absence.

Ratby had begged for leave in order to get rid of his troublesome younger brother.

"I just want to be well rid of him, sir," he had told Anthony, "and if 'e goes to America I can do that. But I 'ave to see him off on the ship meself. Then I'll know 'e's really gone."

Anthony had shrugged and given consent.

Ratby was a most useful partner in crime with an awesome capacity for drink. It was worth giving him the odd indulgence to keep him content in his post.

"Satisfied now?" he asked his valet.

"I saw 'im sail, sir. And I saw somethin' else that may interest you. There's a new shop that's just opened near the dock and you'll never guess who I saw there."

He told his tale. Anthony listened with a cold hard look in his eyes and at last he said,

"Have you mentioned this to anyone else?"

"Nobody, sir."

"Then don't. Here's what I want you to do."

He outlined his plan as Ratby choked with mirth.

"It'll be done, sir, just as you say," he promised.

"Good. First thing tomorrow morning, Ratby, you return to Liverpool."

*

From the window of his office Michael could see the ships entering and leaving the harbour and know that here, in Liverpool, he was living in one of the centres that made England hum with life.

He took care of the bookkeeping for all three shops, bought goods, served from behind the counter and had the satisfaction of seeing his work bear fruit.

He told himself he could make a success of this life.

He would keep Verna locked away into a separate corner of his mind, visiting her now and then and coping with the sadness.

Somehow he would manage.

And then something happened that shattered him.

Looking up one day, he saw a face he recognised.

"Ratby!" he exclaimed in dismay.

"My Lord!"

Ratby came forward with an expression of delight, and wrung Michael's hand.

"Fancy seein' you 'ere! We've all been wonderin' where you were. Some of us've been wishin' you'd come back 'ome."

133

"I cannot come back, Ratby. This is my life now."

"Ah, that's a pity. If you'd returned – well, it's not my place to say – "

"Say what, Ratby?" Michael demanded, alarmed by something in the man's manner. "What is it?"

"Well, like you said, my Lord, you have a new life now. I don't know as 'ow anyone could make a difference for the poor young lady."

"What the devil do you mean? *Tell me!*"

With every sign of reluctance, Ratby told his story. As Michael had feared, it concerned Verna.

"She'll end up by marryin' him, my Lord. She says she won't, but what with 'er father goin' on at her and Mr. Anthony a-pesterin' her – there's nobody to take 'er side, you see, my Lord. She's all on her own. Of course she's a strong young lady and we all know who she really loves, if you'll forgive the liberty, my Lord."

Michael barely heard this last remark.

His mind was filled with nightmare visions of his beloved Verna being forcibly driven towards marriage with Anthony.

She really needed his help desperately and he was not there for her.

"Anthony – " he murmured bitterly.

"Aye sir. I know I shouldn't say this, but I knows 'im better than anyone and 'e's a bad man. It would be different if 'e loved the young lady truly, but 'e doesn't. 'E wants 'er 'cos she was yours. He took everythin' else from you and 'e's determined to 'ave 'er as well. I've even 'eard him say so."

White with shock, Michael stared at him. He had somehow pictured Verna getting on with her life, missing him but surviving. Now he saw that he had abandoned her to persecution and he should have realised.

Ratby, watching his face, accurately judged every thought. Skilfully he tossed more embers onto the fire.

"When 'e's got 'er into his power there's to be no knowin' 'ow 'e'll treat 'er. As 'is wife she'll be 'elpless. Oh, my Lord, why did you go away and abandon 'er?"

"I should never have gone," cried Michael. "How could I do it? My poor Verna! How can I help her?"

"There's only one way, my Lord. If you 'urry back now, you might rescue 'er."

"Yes, yes" he agreed. "That's what I must do."

The door of the shop opened and Henry entered.

He was beaming, but his smile faded when he saw Michael's face.

"Whatever has happened now, Michael? Have our suppliers let us down?"

"Forgive me, Henry, but I must go away for a few days. I cannot explain – but it is very urgent."

Henry nodded kindly.

"Of course. I suppose I knew this would happen."

"But you don't know what has happened."

"Not exactly, but I guess it's something to do with your other existence, isn't it?"

"Yes, it is. Believe me I hate letting you down, but I do really have to go."

"Stay in touch and let me know what's happening," suggested Henry, taking pity on Michael's ravaged face.

Michael thanked him profusely and hurried to pack.

In a few minutes he and Ratby were on their way to the railway station, where they were lucky enough to find a train leaving in half an hour.

During the long journey he asked Ratby some more questions, but did not learn very much more.

He sat back in his seat and closed his eyes.

His mind was seething.

Was it possible that his chance had come? Could he truly rescue Verna and carry her off, marry her and live happily ever after? True, it would be a life of poverty and he had vowed he could never condemn her to that.

But circumstances had changed. Verna was in dire need. Surely anything was better than abandoning her to his brother?

A bright vision rose before him as he journeyed on.

By the time they had reached Halton station it was almost midnight.

He realised that he could not go and see Verna now.

It would mean alerting the whole household and he wanted to snatch the first meeting in private.

He would go and see his brother first.

They took a cab from the station to the house and to his relief there were still lights on.

"Mr. Anthony often sits in the drawin' room late," offered Ratby. "I won't come in, if you don't mind – 'e's going to be annoyed and I'd rather not be there."

He jumped down from the carriage as it drew to a halt and slid away into the darkness.

Michael also climbed down, paid off the driver and stood considering. He did not want to draw any attention to himself.

After a while he began to walk quietly around the house in the darkness, until he saw light coming from the drawing room as the French windows had been left open.

For a while he stood still watching Anthony, who was leaning back on the sofa, his mouth open, snoring. He seemed to be in a drunken stupor.

Going quietly into the room, Michael stood before him, an expression of total contempt on his face.

When Anthony did not move Michael turned away and began to study the room, which had altered since his day.

It was more splendid now. Some valuable antiques had been brought out of storage and displayed in a way he thought excessive. This was something his elegant mother had always refused to do. She had said that only vulgar people puffed off their wealth.

But now the room was like a circus with several pieces he had never seen before, all gleaming gold.

One was a small snuffbox set with diamonds that intrigued him enough to make him pick it up.

"Nice little piece, isn't it?" mumbled a bored voice behind him.

Turning around, Michael could see Anthony rising from the sofa, a triumphant grin on his face.

"Well, well, my long lost brother," he now drawled. "Who would have imagined seeing you again?"

"You should have known I would come back when you started persecuting the lady I love," he replied softly.

"Excuse me? The lady you love? I did not know *tradesmen* were allowed to raise their eyes to ladies! And you are a tradesman now, aren't you? I heard you spend your time serving behind a shop counter."

A faint sensation that something was not quite right stirred an alarm deep within Michael, but he was far too preoccupied to realise that he had walked into a trap.

"I won't bandy words with you," he fumed. "Verna will never be yours."

"You do think so, do you? My dear fellow, you are dreaming. Her father is all for our match."

"Don't tell me that *she* is all for it, because I won't believe you," Michael snapped.

"Oh no, she still feels a certain amount of maidenly reluctance, but on our wedding night it will be my pleasure to overcome it."

He dropped his voice to add,

"I can't tell you how I am looking forward to that."

His words caused a red mist to descend on Michael.

Inside his head he could hear voices bellowing and Verna screaming at him to save her.

The next moment he had launched himself onto his brother in a frenzied attack.

Dimly he became aware that something was out of kilter. Instead of fighting him back, Anthony was simply allowing himself to be punched so that the blood flowed from his nose down his white shirt.

And then it was all over.

Something hard and heavy struck Michael on the back of the head and he collapsed into unconsciousness.

CHAPTER TEN

From her window Verna could see over the gardens to the path where Winifred was standing, gossiping with a young man she did not recognise.

As she watched Winifred whirled and began to run to the house. Every line of her body betrayed agitation.

Verna hurried down to meet her, drawing her into the library.

"Winifred dear, whatever has happened?"

"Such a commotion, you never saw! I always knew he was no good!"

"Who is no good?"

"Lord Belmont, the man who had to leave because he was so bad – "

"Winifred, I forbid you to talk about him like that," Verna corrected her at once. "Michael is *not* bad."

"Wait till you hear what he's done now. He broke into Belmont Park last night and attacked his brother!"

A cold hand seemed to clutch Verna.

"I just don't believe it."

"He tried to steal a solid gold snuff box and when his brother appeared, he attacked him, leaving him covered in blood. If it hadn't been for Ratby, his servant, coming to the rescue, he'd be dead by now."

"I refuse to believe Michael attacked him," Verna stated stubbornly. "It's all a vicious lie."

"Well, he's in a Police cell right this minute," came back Winifred. "Ratby knocked him out and summoned the Police. He's charged with theft and attempted murder."

Verna covered her face in horror.

This was too terrible to be true.

Then she pulled herself together.

"Tell them to bring the car round for me at once. I am going out."

Winifred knew that when Verna spoke in that tone there was no point in arguing.

She sent a message for the car and went to fetch her hat. Wherever Verna went, she was going with her.

In a few minutes they were speeding along the lane towards the village. Verna drove with a set face hiding her inner turmoil.

For months she had yearned for Michael, dreamed of him.

Now the dream had turned into nightmare. If there was even a grain of truth in the story, his life was ruined.

But why? Why had he suddenly returned, yet not contacted her?

"How badly hurt is Anthony?" she asked.

"I wondered when you were going to remember to ask about him. You don't seem to be worried about your fiancé."

"He is *not* my fiancé and he *never* will be!"

"But you do want to know how he is – at least?"

"I want to know for Michael's sake."

"They say he was dreadfully knocked about, but he will recover."

Verna's only response was an agitated cry of,

"Oh, will we never get there?"

"This is not the way to Belmont Park," Winifred suddenly objected.

"I am not going there. I'm going to town."

Once in town she headed for the Police station.

To her infinite relief, she recognised the Sergeant on the desk as the father of one of the Challoner maids.

She had met him several times and he greeted her respectfully.

"Good morning, my Lady. This is an unusual place to see you."

Verna had felt uncertain of how she should behave, but now she made a conscious decision.

Her manner became deliberately haughty.

"I hear you are holding the wretch who is accused of attacking Mr. Anthony Belmont."

"We are indeed, my Lady, and there's no question of his guilt. Theft, burglary, attempted murder, he'll be in prison for the rest of his life."

"I'm glad to hear it," Verna declared, suppressing a desire to scream out in anguish. "Now I want to see him."

"Oh, my Lady, you mustn't go anywhere near him. You wouldn't be safe."

"But I must see this devil. I want to accuse him to his face. Let him look me in the eye, if he can."

The Sergeant looked awkward.

He knew he should not allow this, but deference to the Challoners was second nature to him.

"Just for a few minutes, then. Come through here."

He led her to the back, through a door that led to a narrow corridor where there was the station's only cell.

The door was made entirely of bars and in the poor light she could dimly make out a man sitting on a bed. His clothes were all torn and bloodstained, his face bruised and unshaven.

"Please leave us," she asked tersely.

The Sergeant hesitated.

"It's hardly safe, my Lady," he protested.

But he weakened at the sight of the note in Verna's hand and quickly slipped away.

Left alone Michael and Verna stared at each other in a mixture of joy and horror.

Then they flung themselves against the bars from either side in a vain effort to embrace.

"You came," he murmured. "I was so afraid that you wouldn't – after the things I said to you at our last meeting – about not loving you. *I lied, I lied.*"

"I know," she called passionately. "I always knew. My love, my own love! What are you doing here? What has happened?"

"My dearest Verna," he cried, kissing her as best he could through the bars. "I was a fool. I let myself be taken in by a trick. I should have known better, but I never suspected – "

"What kind of a trick?"

"I've been in Liverpool, working in a shop. I don't know how Ratby found me there, but he came in and began telling me about you and how Anthony was trying to bully you into marrying him.

"I came home at once to stop it. I thought – I don't know really what I thought – that perhaps we might escape together if you still wanted me – "

"If – ? You are all I want in the world. I have told Anthony that I will never marry him. Surely he must have accepted that?"

"He has never accepted that he couldn't have what he wanted," Michael said bitterly. "He's hated me all his life because I was the elder."

"What happened last night?"

"It was dark when I arrived, too late to disturb you. So I went home and found Anthony in the drawing room. I didn't break in, I walked in through the French windows, which were open – purposely as I now recognise.

"We quarrelled and then fought. He spoke of you in such disgraceful terms, so I floored him. Then someone knocked me down from behind. It must have been Ratby.

"I woke up in here to find myself charged with all manner of crimes. The French window had been smashed, there was a gold snuffbox in my pocket and Anthony had far worse injuries than I ever inflicted.

"It was done deliberately. I've been thinking hard, and I realise now that Ratby lured me back on Anthony's orders. While I was lying unconscious, they smashed the window, planted the snuffbox on me and made Anthony's injuries look worse.

"Then Ratby told the Policeman a pack of lies. He denied coming to Liverpool and returning South with me. He said he had been taking a last look around the grounds, seen me breaking in and came to protect his Master."

"But why should Anthony do this?" she wept.

"Because he wants to destroy me utterly. He thinks that way he will win you."

"Never!" she cried vehemently. "I'll never be his, only yours. I'll go and see him now and put a stop to this."

"No, Verna, you must not go. You aren't safe with him. There is nothing he wouldn't do."

"I shall take Winifred with me. Even you are afraid of her. Trust me, my own love. All will be well. We will be together after this."

He gazed at her though the iron bars, his face full of aching and longing.

He loved her so much and he was so fearful for her.

"Together," he whispered. "You and I – *together.*"

"Have faith, dearest love," she told him. "We are meant to be together. It is our destiny. I know it!"

The power with which she said, '*I know it,*' thrilled Michael even in these circumstances.

What an incredible woman she was! How strong, how brave! And how lucky the man who won her!

And yet he was full of dread. He knew, as she did not, how unpleasant his brother could be.

But he forced himself to smile and touch her face with his fingertips. As she turned and left him, he kept the smile on his face until she was out of sight.

Only then, as he stood alone in the darkness, did he let it fade back once again into the blankness of despair.

*

"I have come to see Mr. Belmont," Verna declared to the maid who opened the door of Belmont Park.

The maid nodded. She had been given her orders.

Mr. Anthony was officially at death's door and so could receive no visitors. The only exception to this rule was Lady Verna, who was to be shown up at once.

Winifred managed to follow Verna up the stairs as far as the bedroom door.

But there she was blocked by Ratby.

"I can't allow you in, I'm afraid," he sneered with every appearance of regret. "Orders."

"If you think I'm to let my Lady enter his bedroom without me – " Winifred began, outraged. "It's shocking!"

"It would indeed be shockin' if my Master were not lying 'elpless," sighed Ratby. "But 'e's that badly 'urt –

surely he can be allowed the comfort of a few words with his betrothed?"

"Betrothed!" Winifred snorted. "She's no more his betrothed than I am. She'll never marry him."

A look of viciousness and cunning combined crept over Ratby's face.

"Well, you know. I think she probably will!"

Verna had already slipped past into the bedroom. Now Ratby closed the door behind her, leaving her alone with the figure lying in the bed.

He did not move, but watched as she approached. The curtains were all closed and in the poor light she could not be sure how badly he was hurt.

"Thank you for coming," he croaked at last. "Did you hear what happened?"

"I heard a story that I could hardly believe."

"Believe it. He tried to kill me, Verna. Now he's behind bars where he belongs and where he'll stay for the rest of his life."

She drew a sharp breath.

"No! You cannot do that to him."

"I have no choice in the matter. He must pay for what he has done."

Something in his voice – a hint of smug pleasure – told her that Michael had been right all the time. This was no misunderstanding, but a *vile* trick.

With a swift movement she pulled back the curtains and turned to face him.

In the suddenly brilliant light she saw that his eyes were glittering with vicious pleasure.

"It is true," she breathed. "Everything Michael said – he was right. You lured him back here to trick him."

For a moment she thought he would deny it. But then he shrugged and heaved himself from the bed, pulling on his dressing-gown.

"All right," he admitted. "I tricked him. He came here, just as I meant him to."

"And the rest – he didn't steal from you – or try to kill you – "

"I am very sure he'd have liked to kill me, but no, we did exchange a few punches. Most of my bruises were inflicted by Ratby on my orders after Michael passed out. Then he sent for the Police."

"Anthony, for pity's sake, you cannot do this. It is not too late. You can withdraw the charges – "

"Could I? Yes, I suppose I could – if I was to be *persuaded*."

"And what would it take to persuade you?"

But she knew the answer already. It was there in his face and in the feeling of mounting horror within her.

"No," she screamed. "*No!*"

"Why not? You know I want to marry you. Think of me as a man ready to go to desperate lengths to win the hand of the woman he loves."

"Love! You know *nothing* of love."

"Call it what you will. I want you and I am going to have you by any means possible."

"Never," she yelled violently at him. "I will never marry you."

"Then Michael will stay in prison until he dies."

The casual way he spoke made her want to strike him, but she controlled herself.

Michael's fate depended on what she did now.

"And if I do agree to marry you," she said slowly, "you will order him to be released."

"On the day after our wedding."

"No. He must be released first or no wedding."

"You are hardly in a position to make conditions."

"On the contrary, I will never find myself in such a strong position again. If I marry you first, I won't have a single card to play when you break your word."

"So you don't trust me?"

"That surprises you?" she demanded bitterly. "No, I don't trust you. I *know* you'll go back on your promise if I give you the chance, so I will not give it to you."

"And why should I trust *your* word?"

"Because I am not you," she answered simply.

He considered for a moment and then shrugged.

"All right. We'll compromise. Our engagement is announced, we have a big party. Then I drop the charges and Michael is released."

Verna felt her head spinning.

How could this be happening? She was about to take a step that would break her heart forever, yet she stood here negotiating the complete destruction of her life with as much cool nerve as a duellist going in for the kill.

But she had no choice.

She had said she would do anything for Michael, even die for him. What was being asked was a thousand times worse – not to die – but to live in misery in order to keep him safe.

She would do it.

No matter what it cost, she would do it and count any sacrifice worthwhile as long as she could save him.

"Very well," she said, managing to speak calmly. "When he is safely out of the country – I will marry you."

"Oh, no! He will be here for our wedding. In fact he will be my best man. Then the whole world can see that he and I are friends."

His tone was final and she knew she had negotiated as far as she dared.

"I will – marry you," she muttered in a low voice.

"Good. We will marry and I am certain that we'll be happy once you understand the behaviour I expect from you."

"What?"

She stared at him.

"From this moment you will not attempt to contact Michael again. No secret visits to the Police station. And no letters. If I find out that you have disobeyed me, our agreement is off. Do I make myself clear?"

"Perfectly – clear," she stammered in a dead voice.

"Then let us seal our bargain with a kiss."

He took her in his arms and pulled her close.

"My pretty bride," he murmured, "*my wife* – mine for ever."

She heard no more.

Darkness descended and she collapsed against him.

*

On the night before her wedding Verna sat at her dressing table, staring hopelessly into the mirror.

Could that despairing creature be her? Could those bleak eyes and dead face really be hers?

She was glad to be lifeless. If she had had to feel everything that had happened in the last three weeks, she knew she could not have born it.

It was like watching someone else move through a dream – the announcement of her engagement to Anthony, the grand party at which she had just smiled and smiled, and finally the news that Michael had been released – all charges withdrawn.

She had seen him only once when Anthony came calling, bringing Michael with him for 'a family occasion'.

There had been no chance to speak to him alone, but she had met his eyes, seen the agony that matched her own and known that he understood everything.

In silence they had looked at each other and the air was full of their unspoken goodbyes.

Then they were aware of Anthony watching them, his eyes narrow and spiteful, and they both turned away.

Afterwards Anthony had taken her aside and said,

"You see, *I* have kept my word. He is free. I have kept my side of the bargain, now you must keep *yours*."

"And I will," she told him.

"You know what will happen if you don't – "

He meant that all the charges could be reinstated. Once she was married to him, Anthony could have Michael arrested again and she would have no bargaining card to rescue him.

If only he realised the danger and vanished as soon as the ceremony was over.

She could not see him to warn him, but she did the next best thing by sending a footman in secret to Belmont Park, begging Michael to escape as the bridal party left the Church.

Even so the trick was fraught with danger and she knew no peace until the footman returned to report that the message was delivered and Michael had given his promise.

Now she thought of her wedding only a few hours away. Michael would be the best man, presenting a picture of family unity to the world.

Then he would walk away and she would never see him again.

Verna lay down her head on her arms while many tears streamed down her cheeks.

"Goodbye, Michael, my dear love," she whispered. "Goodbye forever – goodbye – *goodbye* – "

*

Michael too felt as though he was living in some ghastly nightmare as he made the journey to the Church at Anthony's side.

His brother was giving a sickening performance of a happy bridegroom, burbling in a way that made Michael want to strike him. He kept it up during the drive, as they walked into the Church and made their way to the altar.

From the West door came a hum of activity which meant that the bride had arrived. The organ began to play.

Michael braced himself for the moment when he knew he must turn and look at Verna in her bridal gown.

"My bride is here," Anthony whispered gleefully. "Look at her. Isn't she ravishing? Did you ever see such a beautiful woman?"

Michael flung his brother a look of loathing. But at last he forced himself to turn his head and watch Verna approaching on her father's arm.

She was, as Anthony had implied, the very picture of beauty – tall and elegant, her slim body attired in white satin, a long veil streaming down to the floor behind her.

With anguish he recalled how he had once dreamed of this very scene, how he would stand here, watching her walk down the aisle towards him.

But in his dreams that had been their own wedding. *He* was the groom and not Anthony. Now here they were, going through the same motions, but how different.

How horribly different!

The pain was unbearable.

"Have you got the ring?" Anthony demanded.

"Of course I have it."

"Good. I don't want anything to go wrong. That would be disrespectful to Verna. She is a very particular young woman, likes everything to be 'just so'. And I aim to please her in every respect – not that I think she'll have any complaints."

He said the last words with a lascivious leer that made Michael want to kill him – the thought of his darling helpless in the hands on this swine was more than he could bear.

Watching Michael as she neared him, Verna saw everything – his pain, his defiance, his bewilderment that their love had come to this.

She had no doubt that the years ahead would be wretched. Anthony claimed to love her, but in truth he felt only desire and a kind of hate that she had resisted him.

He had been so certain that she would fall into his arms once Michael had gone and when she did not, he had become hostile.

He would force her to become his wife and then he would crush her.

Nearer and nearer she trod, her intense gaze fixed on Michael's face, her eyes full of the message that must remain forever silent.

'I love you – I love you – in all my life there will be no one but you – *I love you* – '

Michael saw and understood all that she could not put into words. He knew that her heart cried out to him in the moment of final parting and his cried out in return.

Now she was here.

With an insufferably smug expression on his face Anthony reached for her, planted a kiss on her cheek and drew her forward to stand beside him.

The Vicar appeared ready to conduct the wedding. He smiled at the bride and groom.

But before he could say a single word, the peace of the Church was shattered by a bellow of pain and rage.

"*There you are, damn you! I've got you at last.*"

Shocked, everyone looked around for the source of the noise.

A young man was advancing down the aisle.

He was in his early twenties with a rough shabby appearance and several days' growth of beard.

But what held everyone frozen with horror was the gun in his hands.

Some of the guests began to step forward, meaning to stop him, but the sight of the gun made them pause, then fall back.

"*You!*"

The man stopped in front of Anthony.

"You thought you could get away from me. I've seen you slithering and sliding away, desperate not to let me see you."

"I don't know what you're talking about," Anthony responded in a voice with a slightly hysterical edge. "Who are you, fellow? I don't know you."

"Oh, you know me all right. You've been running away from me for weeks, ever since I found out what you did to my poor Maria. Or are you going to pretend you've never heard of her too?"

Anthony made one further attempt at lofty scorn.

"I really cannot be expected to recall the name of every servant girl – "

He stopped as the man came closer and waved the gun in his face.

"Every servant girl you've *seduced*?"

"I – I – "

"Let's see if I can refresh your memory – I'm Frank Buller that used to work in your stables. Maria was my promised bride till you set eyes on her. After that she was lost. Do you think I don't know all you did to dazzle the poor sweet girl until you'd lured her into your bed?"

There was a low murmur of consternation from the congregation.

Anthony's face became puce.

"That is all a perverse wicked lie," he blustered. "I know nothing of this woman – "

"You left her with child," Buller screamed. "And then you disowned her. She begged you for help, but you abandoned her so that she ran away to hide her shame.

"I searched for her high and low, and at last I found her alone, starving, about to give birth. She bore her child, but it was dead and an hour later she too died in my arms.

"I promised her I would find the bastard who did this to her and make him pay for all his wickedness. And that's what I'm here to do!"

He advanced on Anthony who had gone very pale.

"You must be mad," he choked, "thinking you can turn up here on my wedding day – "

"*Your* wedding day," snarled Buller. "You should have made an honest woman of my Maria – "

Anthony was rash enough to let a sneer overtake his face.

Buller saw it and started forward.

"You killed her," he shrieked madly. "You tricked her into your bed with false promises and threw her away when you had no further use for her."

153

"She was m-mad," Anthony stammered. "Thinking a gentleman in my p-position could m-marry her. She was out of her mind to imagine it."

"Oh, poor soul," whispered Verna, burying her face in her hands. "Poor soul. Was there nobody to help her?"

"She was well paid," Anthony yelped. "She should have known her place. You cannot blame me."

"She loved you!" shrieked Buller. "She died loving you and I held her body in my arms and vowed to avenge her. And that's what I'm going to do!"

He cried aloud to the Heavens.

"*I do this for you, Maria.*"

At that moment life returned into Michael's limbs. Until then he had stood frozen with horror barely able to take in what was happening.

But, when he saw the gun aimed at Anthony, every thought left him except that this was his brother.

Barely knowing what he did, he launched himself forward, knocking Anthony to the ground and out of the way of the shot.

There were screams from the congregation as a shot rang out, but he barely heard them.

A sword of fire pierced his shoulder, torturing him with pain and making him groan.

He could now feel Anthony moving beneath him, shoving him brutally aside so that more pain savaged him.

From somewhere came Buller's cry,

"Don't think you can escape me – "

Then another blast split the air and there was more screaming as Anthony's body crashed to earth beside him.

Verna dropped to her knees, sobbing,

"Oh, my love – my love – " reaching out to the man who lay there bleeding.

A murmur of horror ran around the Church.

Most of the congregation thought how terrible for her that Verna should witness her groom lying beside her covered in blood.

But the more observant amongst them noticed that the man she was cradling in her arms was not her groom.

*

Michael's shoulder pounded with agony.

The doctor's words were reassuring,

"Only a flesh wound – no permanent damage."

But the pain hammered on and on, until eventually a large dose of morphine took effect and he could sleep.

When he woke many hours later, he could only just make out Verna leaning over him.

She had changed from her wedding dress and into a sober gown of grey and her face was terribly pale.

But she was still beautiful, he thought hazily.

"Thank God you are now awake," she murmured ardently. "I've been so afraid you would die – "

"He isn't going to die," came the doctor's voice. "I keep promising you that. I'll call again tomorrow."

He left the room and Verna and Michael looked at each other.

"Anthony?" he groaned.

"Anthony is dead. Buller fired again – and it went straight through his heart."

They were silent, holding hands.

"You tried to save him," she whispered.

"He is my brother."

"And you are the most generous man in the world," she sighed in a wondering voice. "After everything he did to you – "

"I know. But I couldn't just stand aside and let him die."

He slept for a while and when he woke up his sister Jane was sitting on his bed.

"Ask Verna to come and see me," he murmured.

"She isn't here, Michael. She's returned to her own home, but she says she will be back later."

"Her home? But isn't this – ? No – wait."

"Everything was prepared for her to become the Mistress of this house," Jane answered, "but Anthony died before the wedding could take place."

She was looking at him significantly, but his brain was still cloudy and he could not be sure what she meant.

*

Verna looked up as a middle-aged man with a tired look entered the drawing room of Challoner Abbey.

"Mr. Tanway," she said, smiling as she recognised the family lawyer. "Have you come to see my father?"

"No, I need to speak to you," he replied in his reedy voice. "I am afraid I have bad news for you."

Her heart sank into her boots, but she maintained a calm appearance as she led him into the drawing room.

"Please tell me the worst, Mr. Tanway. What has happened?"

"The worst news is that you were very nearly a rich widow. Anthony's death was a tragedy, of course – " he did not sound as if he considered it at all sad, "but if only he had died a few minutes later, you would have been his wife and inherited his considerable wealth.

"As it is, the Reverend Elvan is adamant that the marriage ceremony had not even begun, which means that Mr. Belmont died a bachelor and his wealth will be now inherited by that no-good brother of his."

"Do you mean Michael – Lord Belmont?" Verna asked in a strangled voice.

"That's him. All the good work I did, negotiating a will that would have left you very rich, all came to nothing because he died too soon. You were not married and he was not due to sign his new will until after the ceremony."

"Are you certain that Michael is his heir?"

"Oh, yes," he sighed. "Anthony had never made a previous will, and, as his elder brother, Lord Belmont is his next of kin. He gets everything."

He gave a melancholy lawyerly sigh.

Verna could tell that Mr. Tanway had completely misunderstood her. He thought she was pining for the loss of money, whereas she was ecstatic that Michael would at last inherit what was rightfully his.

And in some secret place, deep within herself, she was full of joy that the marriage had never taken place.

A man could not marry his brother's widow – that was against the law. And if she had been Anthony's wife, she could never be Michael's.

Now that shadow was lifted from her.

Lord Challoner came in a few minutes later to find Verna ready to leave.

"I'm going, Papa," she said. "I'll stay with Michael while he is ill, then I will marry him, if he will have me. Please don't oppose me as I shall not obey you."

But her father had no intention of opposing her. He too had spoken to the lawyer and knew that Michael was now a rich man as well as the Earl.

His attitude had adjusted to the changed situation.

"I'll drive you there myself, my dear," he beamed.

Winifred insisted on coming too, sitting in the back like a protective dragon, as she had so often done before.

But this time the dragon was firmly on Michael's side. Just let anyone try to come between him and Verna. They would have Winifred to deal with!

At Belmont Park Michael's sisters were crowded at the front door to welcome Verna.

"We were so afraid you wouldn't come back," cried Jane. "You won't go away again, will you?"

"No, I have come to stay," Verna replied firmly. "This time I am not risking anything going wrong. Will you take me to him?"

Michael heard the sound of voices coming up the stairs and struggled up in his bed.

'Verna,' he muttered, 'I must see her.'

The next moment his bedroom door burst open and Verna ran in, arms open wide to embrace him. He reached for her and they fell back on the bed together.

"Is it you?" he whispered. "Are you really here?"

"Yes, my dear beloved. I am here and I am going to stay here with you for ever and ever. We are going to be married and nothing is going to stand in our way."

"Is Anthony really dead or did I dream it?"

"Yes, Buller killed him and then he killed himself. It's all over now."

"Ratby – " Michael queried suddenly.

"Nobody has seen him. He must have run away."

"Very wise of him."

"The lawyer says that you are now Anthony's heir," Verna told him, "and as I was never his wife, there can be no impediment to my becoming yours."

He stared at her horrified as he finally understood the danger they had narrowly escaped.

"A few minutes later and we would not have been able to marry – ever," he mumbled.

"Yes. But now we can. Oh, Michael, I am so glad you have your rightful inheritance, but I would marry you without a penny. I care nothing for money, only for *you*."

"I should have married you all those months ago, Verna, when you were so brave and strong. You were so right and I should have listened."

"Yes, you should. And in future I'm going to make *sure* that you always listen to me!"

He gave a faint smile.

"Am I going to live under the cat's paw?"

"Under all four of them. Your wife will bully you, and order you around and remind you constantly that she knows best!"

"And will she kiss me and love me?"

"All the time!"

"That's all right then. She can bully me as much as she likes as long as she is there holding me all night."

"Oh, my love, I am a shameless creature," Verna exclaimed, half laughing, half weeping. "Look at me lying here with you. I am so compromised, but I don't care if it means you have to marry me."

"Nothing will stop me," he vowed. "Must we wait a decent interval?"

She shook her head.

"No, we will take no chances. Nothing matters but to be together. If people want to gossip, let them gossip, as long as you are mine and I am yours."

"You are right," he muttered, closing his eyes and resting his head against her.

"You are mine and I am yours. And thank God for His boundless goodness in bringing us together at last. It is Love, Michael, Love Eternal for ever and ever."

Anthony was buried during the following week and the wedding took place a month later.

The Church was crammed with their relatives and friends. And there in a place of honour was Henry and his family, thrilled at the marriage of 'their' Michael.

For he had no wish to sever his ties with Liverpool. On the contrary he had invested generously in the business, enabling Henry to branch out with a fourth store.

Henry nearly burst with pride. Business partner to an Earl! Just wait until his rivals heard about it!

But although all eyes were fixed on them, the bride and groom had no eyes for anyone but each other.

As they came together at the altar, the world around them vanished.

Only their love mattered, the undying love that had sustained them through so many trials and tribulations.

And would continue to strengthen them and bring them endless joy through the years ahead.

When the Vicar asked them if they took each other, their lips responded with the conventional words, but their hearts cried out a thousand passionate vows.

They had been through fire and hell and now they knew that their love was powerful enough to light up a new and everlasting world.

That world was waiting for them in all its glory as they turned to walk back down the aisle and out into the brilliant sunshine.